"They were right," he said in English. "An exceptionally beautiful specimen."

"Don't," she said.

"You resist me?" He seemed amused.

A horrible fascination seized her as she felt his hand move slowly down her cheek to caress her neck, her shoulders, her arms. "Tell me, what is a woman like you doing in a remote part of Japan, one that was raided precisely because no one thought it would contain anyone from outside, a village my strategists convinced me could be made to disappear unnoticed?"

Something about the way he stared at her . . . Suddenly it hit her: *a lizard is going to make love to me*, she thought, *and then I'm going to be killed!*

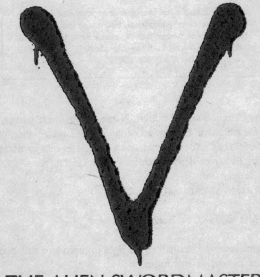

THE ALIEN SWORDMASTER

Somtow Sucharitkul

PINNACLE BOOKS   NEW YORK

V: THE ALIEN SWORDMASTER

Copyright © 1985 by Warner Bros., Inc.

An original Pinnacle Books edition, published for the first time
anywhere.

First printing/April 1985

ISBN: 0-523-42441-8
Can. ISBN: 0-523-43421-9

Printed in the United States of America

PINNACLE BOOKS, INC.
1430 Broadway
New York, New York 10018

9   8   7   6   5   4   3   2   1

To the Chan family,
whose cooking sustained me through
this book,
and to Michael Dirda,
whose laughter didn't hurt either,
and to Chris Baer,
who has two Visitors in his bedroom!

PART ONE

LIBERATION: TOKYO

Chapter 1

Darkness: lisping, hissing, metal-tinged voices from reptile tongues. An alien speech: guttural, grating, incomprehensible.

Cold. Dark. Frozen. Barely breathing. Unable to move. There were restraints around her limbs, her waist. It was like a nightmare where you were bound so tightly you couldn't breathe, couldn't move, couldn't even wake up. *Where am I?* she thought. Something spongy, bulbous brushed against her face. She tried to open her eyes, her eyelids struggling against whatever it was—drugs? a force field?—but she couldn't force them open. Again the wet, nasty, cold thing slithering across her face, tendriling around, like the caress of a serpent lover. *Jesus God, let me wake up,* she thought. *Let me wake up!*

Voices again. She strained to hear; they seemed infinitely far away. They drifted in and out of her consciousness, buzzing, buzzing.

Once more she fought the thing that kept her in her frozen bondage. But it was too much. *My metabolism must have gone weird or something,* she thought. In the cold, dark silence she could sense her heart beating, pitapat . . . pitapat—too slow! *If this was a nightmare and I was this scared, I'd have adrenaline racing in my bloodstream; my heart would be pounding, pounding.* It had to be some kind of drug then, pushing her down, down into this lethargy.

3

What were these *things* clambering over her body then? Electrodes? No. They teased the edge of her numbness. . . . Tubes. *Like ones used for saline solution or intravenous feeding, like the ones in a hospital maybe. Am I sick?* She fished around in her memory but kept coming up empty. Except for—

Eyes.

Glaring, glowering lizard eyes; slitty, topaz colored, merciless.

Where were they coming from?

Abruptly, the voices returned, much nearer, still incomprehensible. Then one of them snapped in a language she recognized, "Enough of this! We're to keep up the illusion at all times, don't you understand? None of this home-planet talk. We're to speak Earth tongues or shut up. Practice makes perfect."

Yes. She understood the language well enough. As an infant she'd learned it from her mother, and then she'd taken it in college. And then, of course, as part of her field training, she'd—

"What illusion?" Another voice, perhaps female. "Don't you think it's rather pointless to be keeping up illusions in front of the food? I mean, there's such a thing as too much caution."

Why couldn't she see? More gibberish followed, then a hideous hissing that returned the conversation to the Japanese language.

"Turn on the light, someone." A red glow in front of her closed eyes. "What about that one there?"

"I don't think the leader wants a boy tonight."

"Oh. I can't tell the difference myself. Ugly, hairy things!"

"There is something to them, though. Sometimes I look at myself in a mirror. I'm in my dermoplast suit and the alien sunlight falls on these imitated features and I think, not bad you know, not bad. So what if I look like an ape? They're very streamlined. Have you ever seen them swimming? The light just glances off their slippery backs. Then the water cascades down their scaleless skin and trickles, shining, down their smooth limbs. You can see their muscles ripple under that strange translucent skin. If you ask me, it's pretty attractive in a bizarre sort of way."

"Shut up. You're making me hungry."

Suddenly a flash of memory.

The Ainu village. The shuttlecraft falling from the sky. The screaming villagers banging down the door of the institute headquarters . . .

"Food! Is that all you ever think of?"

"What about you and your insatiable lusts? If we stopped to couple with every alien life form we conquered, do you think we'd be ruling this quadrant of the galaxy? No. These apes'd probably be in charge and then where would you be? I was down at one of the Indonesian headquarters, and you know what I saw? One of these aliens spitting and roasting a big lizard of some kind, a Komodo dragon they call it. It looked so much like one of my own children back on the home world. I felt like lasering him to death right then and there, but oh, no, we're supposed to—"

"Keep up the illusions. Yes." They relapsed into more gibberish for a moment, and she remembered. . . .

Herding the humans into a great big pen, the infants squalling, the old women clasping and unclasping their hands, the men dull-eyed, defeated, falling in like cattle, and she was coming out of the institute with Professor Schwabauer to see what all the fuss was about when one of the red-uniformed Visitors barked at them and told them, "Get in line, human scum!" and they were caught up in the crowd and propelled forward, unable to resist, and Schwabauer muttering all the time, "I want to see the *verdammte* German consul. We're part of an international anthropological team. I want you to call Zimmerman. You know Zimmerman, the German consul in Sapporo, or call the Embassy in Tokyo. I protest, I protest—" Only to be shoved roughly into the crowd.

"What about this one?"

"Too narrow in the hips. The leader is very particular tonight."

"Well, you know best, I suppose. You're the one that's always having fantasies about the food. Bestiality, I call it."

"Well, they *are* sentient."

"*Sentient!* What kind of an attitude is that? I've half a mind to report you to the attitude-adjustment committee. I mean it's all very well for those softhearted underground religions to nurture such thoughts, but this is a military operation."

"Oh? I had imagined it was more like a trip to the gourmet supermarket."

"Oh, be quiet and let's get on with the job. What about that one?"

A tearing sound. Something was being ripped open right near her skin. She felt a gust of wind, even chillier than the cold that had cocooned her before, then more sounds, like ripping Velcro.

"Not bad. Let's take a good look. Yes, it's the right sex."

"How can you tell?"

"They have very pronounced secondary sex characteristics. Surely you've noticed the protuberances on your disguise? You're supposed to be a female. Look, see? They match." Someone was yanking the tubes off her now. "Listen, kid. You been off-world as long as me, you won't stand around lecturing people on correct military procedure and proper attitudes and rules about not coupling with the aliens. It's a wide, wide galaxy. Just be glad we're the conquerors and have all the privileges. And learn to appreciate the aliens."

"I do! Extremely rare, with just a hint of *kranjosh* seasoning."

"Insufferable cadet arrogance. Yes, I think she'll do very nicely. She's young—"

"How can you tell?"

"Their skin gets wrinkled as they grow older. Good

muscle tone; she'll give our leader a good time, I'm sure, and perhaps he won't drive his poor crew so hard. And . . ." Rough fingers touched her eyelids, forcing them open. She saw at last, the light hurting her eyes. She couldn't focus. "Attractive eyes: greenish-gray. Good. High cheekbones. Long hair, jet-black. Very pale skin. Part Caucasian, I would imagine. She'll do very nicely. Revive and prepare her. He wants to be entertained right after dinner."

"Not during?" A disappointed tone. At last she could see them: first the red uniforms, the not-quite-swastika insignia. A stab in her arm—some kind of injection. She saw she was naked; her arms flew up to cover herself. Two Visitors, a man and a woman. Solemn Asian faces. The woman's was cruel, the mouth twisted in a sardonic smile. The man's seemed a bit more mellow, maybe; she couldn't tell.

She turned.

The room—metal walls, tubes and piping everywhere, and spongy sacks hanging from the walls and suspended from the ceilings, stacked up on shelves. And in the sacks . . .

People. Naked, eyes closed . . . not dead! The feeding tubes wound around the sacks and snaked into the corners. The sacks were like membranes, like . . . placentas. The people drew their slow, collective breath in a steady rhythm as though controlled by some machine.

It came to her suddenly what this was. The rumors she'd heard were true, then. Even worse than true. And why were they reviving her? She looked at her captors. She screamed suddenly, screamed until her throat was raw. Her screaming echoed along the cavernous walls of the metal chamber. And then, abruptly, the scream died. She couldn't go on. Her throat was parched and raspy, and she was so weak. . . .

"*Namae wa nan da?*" said the man.

Something in her snapped. Goddamn it, if I'm going to be eaten, I'm not going to be forced to speak Japanese.

Memories of being teased in school surfaced suddenly from long ago. *"Amerikajin da yo!"* she said angrily. *"Nihongo ga dekinai!"*

The two looked at each other strangely. One said something in the hissing tongue. She couldn't understand it, but it sounded terribly obscene, the way everything in their language did. Then the man said, "So you are American?"

"Yes. I'm with the international anthropological team. We're studying the Ainu, the Caucasiform aboriginal population of the north of Japan. We've been stationed in Hokkaido since . . . since before . . ."

"The invasion," the male Visitor finished for her. "No need to mince words, I suppose." The female stared at them both; clearly she had not been taught English. "Well, you may count yourself lucky, uh . . ."

"Jones. Tomoko Jones."

"Tomoko? You are half Japanese?"

"I'm an American."

"Be that as it may, you have at least temporarily escaped the fate that awaits these others." She shuddered. He went on, "You are about to be taken into the presence of Fieh Chan, the supreme commander of the Mother Ships in the Tokyo–Seoul–Hong Kong sector. I trust you will conduct yourself equitably and perhaps earn your freedom."

"What if I don't?" she said defiantly.

"Then, alas. . . . ." The man gestured at the others, hanging in their womblike sacks.

Chapter 2

She felt numb as they led her down the corridors of what she now realized must be a Visitor Mother Ship. They walked past massive steel doors, some of them with windows through which she caught glimpses of the aliens. Once or twice she saw one of the unmasked reptile faces; quickly she looked away. Once she saw into a storage chamber such as the one she had come from. She shuddered.

At last they reached a large chamber smelling of sandalwood. The floor was lined with tatami matting. A futon bed had been made up on the floor; cushions rested against the wall. No harsh mirror metal here, but bamboo screens and silken tapestries. A *yukata*, or Japanese sleeping robe, was laid out by the bed. Since they had not allowed her the dignity of any kind of garment since reviving her from cold storage, she immediately put it on. As always, she felt a momentary embarrassment because she was too tall and the robe fell awkwardly down to her midcalf.

"Wait here," one said, and they left her alone to meditate her coming fate.

She thought about Matt. She hadn't thought of him in years, but something made her remember the last time she had been face to face with her husband. The memory was stridently clear suddenly.

Standing outside the martial arts studio in Orange County, California, in the burning haze of a terrible heat wave . . . he had been shouting at her. "So get out! Go and look for your roots or whatever. I'm tired of listening to you, it sounds like a damn soap opera. Go to Japan. It's not going to make you happier, but at least I won't have to take your bitching anymore."

"You're not being fair, Matt," she had said. She knew she was hurting him, but something impelled her. She had to leave it all behind: the shiny new car, the house, the pool, that coffeemaker with the microprocessor chip that knew what time you were going to wake up, the glamorous but dull job, the handsome, virile husband. "Professor Schwabauer needs an assistant, and I *do* have an anthropology degree."

"So what? You've never shown any interest in it since I've known you."

"All of six months." He was such a baby sometimes. "Well, I can more or less speak Japanese." Although, she reminded herself, she could hardly remember her own mother. "It's not forever anyways. Just . . . well, nine or ten months."

She remembered him standing there, not quite believing she was actually going to do it. *God, he's good-looking,* she remembered thinking, *and so considerate. Until now.* "I'm doing it, Matt," she said, feeling empty and brutal suddenly. Even though she'd already talked the whole thing through with her analyst. "Just nine months."

Nine months. . . .

But then the Visitors had come.

She remembered it vividly; Schwabauer had come to fetch her. They were going to catch the bullet train. From Tokyo they would go north to Hokkaido island where the primitive Ainu, blue-eyed and white-skinned, lived. A veritable gold mine for anthropologists, Schwabauer had told her.

The train had just begun to pull out. Tokyo underground

was as labyrinthine and vast as Tokyo aboveground. The train was slowly chugging through the tunnels, and they were settling down to a *bento* packaged lunch of raw fish on sesame rice when suddenly (almost like being born, she remembered thinking) they shot out into the sunlight somewhere in the suburbs. Only, it wasn't sunlight, because this tremendous *thing* was blotting out the sun.

Later she remembered watching it all on TV: the arrival, the UN address, the whole thing. Then came the restrictions. Necessary, they said. You couldn't get clearance to leave the country. She called Matt once a month for a while, but it always seemed to deteriorate into an argument.

She threw herself into her work. After all, what difference did all this interplanetary politics make? So what if there were alien advisers in the Japanese cabinet?

Then there were the rumors about the Visitors being reptiles, followed by that dramatic TV exposure. They'd managed to catch that broadcast from America for a few moments before it was squelched by a blackout from Tokyo. Even then, Tomoko thought, *People or lizards, what does it matter?* An anthropologist knows better than to judge by appearances. She found herself curiously unmoved at the thought that the aliens were reptiles. After all, she'd read science fiction when she was a kid. She knew that the possibilities of a hundred percent humanoid race evolving on another world were pretty remote, not to mention the possibility that they would happen to be the first extraterrestrial civilization humans would encounter. Live and let live, she'd thought. After all, they weren't doing any harm, and they were giving the human race quite a bit of their technology. As for the rumor that they were capturing people and salting them away for planetside consumption, she thought that was just typical human chauvinism. Just another sci-fi cliché. She'd seen it on *The Twilight Zone*, for God's sake! "To Serve Man," that was the name of the episode.

Then they raided the village, and she woke up trussed and

hanging on a meat rack in a gelatinous basket being bathed in bizarre juices—for all she knew being marinated or something!—and she knew this wasn't a TV series or a bad dream. It was for real . . . they ate people.

How long had she been in the cold sleep? Years? And what would happen now? They had mentioned the name of Fieh Chan, spoken of him in hushed, mantralike tones. She'd heard of him before, even seen him on TV. He was the wise and glorious leader of the Visitors in this particular sector of the earth. But if he was the leader of the creatures who'd raided her village, he wasn't so wise and glorious, was he? If he was one of them, he must eat people too.

And here I am, waiting for him, like an enticing tidbit. . . .

A hand on her shoulder.

She jumped. A scream died on her lips. She saw his face only a few inches from her own. She recognized him at once; who wouldn't? His was the most famous face in this part of the world.

He looked at her very seriously. His mask was that of a vigorous older man with graying hair, fastidiously combed. He watched her for a long time, until she felt as though his eyes were boring right through her. She winced as he reached out to toy with a strand of her hair.

"They were right," he said in English. "An exceptionally beautiful specimen." He had a slight trace of a British accent, and even though she knew it was stupid, she couldn't help feeling a bit inferior because of it.

"Don't," she said.

"You resist me?" He seemed amused.

"Do I have a choice?" she said bitterly.

"No." He studied her for a moment, his lips twitching.

A horrible fascination seized her as she felt his hand move slowly down her cheek to caress her neck, her shoulders, her arms. "Tell me, what is a woman like you doing in a remote part of Japan, one that was raided precisely because no one thought it would contain anyone from outside, a village that my strategists convinced me could be made to disappear unnoticed?''

Something about the way he stared at her . . . Suddenly it hit her: *a lizard is going to make love to me,* she thought, *and then I'm going to be killed!* Conflicting feelings whirled through her mind. She couldn't control herself anymore. It all started to gush from her lips, all of it: her childhood identity crisis, her marriage to the handsome, macho martial arts expert with the overpriced karate school in the suburbs, her recent obsession with roots. *What's the matter with me?* she thought angrily. *What's come over me to make me bare my soul to an alien from another planet?* She was thinking, castigating herself even as she poured out all her inner turmoil.

Chapter 3

At last she was through. Exhausted from her warring emotions, she sank down onto the futon bed. There was a low bedside table with a lacquered surface; a couple of tea bowls, all the utensils for the traditional tea ceremony. Against one wall was a Japanese-style shrine with an image of Buddha; it was clearly a costly antique. Her trained mind identified it as a seventeeth century object. To her surprise, Fieh Chan squatted down at the table and began to pour tea, his wrist crooked at the elegantly correct angle. After a moment's meditation he handed her a bowl of fragrant green tea. "This will make you feel better." He did not look at her. "You are surprised by my gentleness? I, the ruthless conqueror?"

"You are Fieh Chan," she said, trembling inwardly. "Once I saw on the news you commanded that an entire town be put to death."

"Yet I too am a creature of two worlds. I too am tormented. Can you believe that?"

"I know better than to think of anyone, human or alien, as one dimensional. Professor Schwabauer's training—"

"Let me show you something about power," Fieh Chan said, rising abruptly. He clapped his hands.

Suddenly the *shoji* walls were flung aside, and the bamboo screens were pulled up into the ceiling. They were now looking out on to a panoramic view of a great city.

Skyscrapers sprouted in wild confusion, neon signs glittered, skywalks stitched the buildings. In the distance stood an exact copy of the Eiffel Tower, except that it was red instead of green. Cars crowded the streets and people thronged the sidewalks. It was the bustling metropolis of Tokyo.

"Look closer, Tomoko," said Fieh Chan, drawing her up from the futon and making her stand with her nose almost touching the viewscreen. "The screens give a perfect illusion, don't they? Look. Do you see that circlet of shadow that has engulfed the center of the city, the Ginza area?" She saw it then: a patch of darkness too regular in shape to be the shadow of a cloud. It had swallowed up the Takashimaya department store, the Tokyu Building, even . . . "Yes, that little piece of Americana too, the McDonald's at the corner of the Ginza. And do you know what is casting the shadow?"

She nodded numbly.

"Yes. Our Mother Ship! That is what power is all about, Tomoko! Do you wonder that I am troubled? But I must obey."

"Why are you telling me all this?"

"Why not? They tell me I have a habit of rambling, of trying to justify myself, before I indulge my . . . ah . . . Anyway, there's no danger in it."

"You can always have me killed," Tomoko said bitterly.

"Or converted. Doubtless you've heard of our conversion chambers. Yes, we can take away your mind and substitute something fanatically subservient, soulless, utterly loyal." She shuddered and gazed out at the city. When she looked more closely, she could see that some buildings had been blasted down to rubble, that large segments of the city had been reduced to fields of broken concrete.

"It has not been easy to hold on to this part of the world," Fieh Chan said sadly. "The Japanese in particular seem not to fear death, and there have been constant kamikaze attacks on our mission in the Ginza."

"What did you expect? Slavish devotion?" *They're going to kill me anyway,* she thought. *I'll say anything I want.*

"I did not expect to have to reduce this city to ruins. Oh, I need to forget," Fieh Chan said. His eyes shone, but their luster was an alien luster, hinting of a cold citrine fire. "And you are a beautiful woman. My lieutenant chose well."

"Beautiful! How could you know? We are aliens. Oh, I overheard them discussing me like a piece of steak. 'Ugly, hairy things,' one of them said of us. What do you see in us anyway?"

"There is a myth among us, Tomoko," he said, his eyes far away. "It is said that once the apelike creatures ruled our world, much as the dinosaurs once ruled yours. The myth says that before the dawn of civilization there was a great war and the race of apes was cast down and became dumb. Of course, it's just a story. But you can see why your race is so fascinating to us. On the one hand, you're a ludicrous obscenity—talking apes, how could such a thing be possible? —and on the other, your existence makes us yearn for a world that is no more, the golden age before we became warlike. But what I speak is heresy. You will not repeat it."

"No. I will not," Tomoko said, becoming more and more drawn to him, though she knew that his artificial skin hid serpent scales and an alien mind. There was something attractive about him; his very vulnerability. Matt had always been so unyielding, so full of that endless male ego.

"Are you thinking, perhaps you should be faithful to your husband? He is a karate teacher, you told me?"

"More than that. He's an expert at a dozen kinds of martial arts. He's one of the best in the country, actually. He was in *People* magazine once."

"You are proud of him."

"I guess so." She thought of the endless round of dull tournaments and the walls and walls of glittering trophies, and the number of times she'd screamed at him about it.

What was he doing now? Was he stuck in some meat locker in Los Angeles?

"But you see, you are attracted to me also," he said. "It is mutual."

"I do not see your true face," she said.

"But you know it. You sense it. I am the serpent in your garden. Yes, we too have such legends. The temptress ape that embodies all that would drag us down from our pinnacle of civilization. Yes!" he whispered harshly, a tinge of echoing metal in his voice. "That is why we must crush you, devour your kind, rape you, commit acts of savagery upon you! For we must never face the fact that you may be as intelligent as ourselves. It would destroy the very fabric of our beliefs and the archetypal mysteries of our minds!"

"Yes," she said. She had always known from her anthropological studies that the images of man and serpent were inextricably linked in the human consciousness, all through history, perhaps even before men evolved. Chimpanzees, she recalled from her lab work, will recoil in revulsion from a snake in a manner way out of proportion to the possible danger. But in that racial horror—mutual, she had now learned—there was also fascination, also mutual. Each race seemed to represent for the other all that was base about the human or reptilian condition. *But how can I be thinking of such things now?* she thought. *Jesus, I'm standing here in the lizard's lair writing a doctoral thesis in my head when I should be screaming in terror!* Wildly she looked around for an avenue of escape, knowing it was hopeless—

He seized her in his arms. She was taller than he was. Those eyes again, transfixing her, hypnotizing her. *Oh God,* she thought, *I'm going to kiss him, and I think I may even like it.*

Suddenly an alarm sounded.

The screens that had been showing the panorama of Tokyo suddenly blanked out. Fieh Chan barked something in his metallic alien voice. "What's going on?" she cried.

Screams came from outside, shouts, reptilian shrieks, sounds of panic.

"What's the matter?" she screamed again.

"What's the matter?" Fieh Chan grated. "Behold!"

She stared at the viewscreens; now they were cutting rapidly from scene to scene.

She saw balloons flying through the air, trailing clouds of red dust.

In the interior of another spacecraft, Visitors were collapsing, tearing off their human faces and showing the slitty-eyed, green-scaled horrors beneath. A close-up of a screaming reptile showed his flesh melting hideously. "Diana's ship!" Fieh Chan said. "They've managed to infiltrate the high command itself!"

A voice rang out over the hubbub: "Fieh Chan, we estimate that the toxic dust will reach Japan in approximately two hours—perhaps even sooner! Trace amounts are in the air already. Many of our crew members are succumbling."

On the screen now, shots of Mother Ships bucking against Earth's atmosphere, bursting into the stratosphere.

"Quick! We must escape!" Fieh Chan said urgently. "Follow me or I'll be dead. And then I won't be able to answer for your safety!"

He grabbed her by the hand and went to the shrine in the wall niche. He lifted the Buddha image she had been admiring earlier. Suddenly the wall gave way and—

They were standing in a loading dock. A sleek shuttlecraft gleamed. "We've no time! Climb in!" Fieh Chan said.

A wild thought—*I'm still in my sleeping robe!*—and then she clambered into the cramped little craft. Fieh Chan followed her and pressed some controls on a console. "Have to seal off every possible vent or the toxin will get in." She marveled at how logically he was acting under the stress. "Strap yourself in! Get a grip on yourself!"

"What does this mean, this toxin? What's happening?"

"What does it mean?" The purr of the shuttlecraft

revving up for takeoff. "It means we're finished—that our reign on Earth is over! Your resistance has cooked up something that can kill us, can't you see? Now be quiet or I'll never be able to get this thing out of here."

She clutched her *yukata* robe hard to herself. "Freedom?" she said softly.

"Yes, freedom!" Fieh Chan said, his voice sounding infinitely weary. "But for me . . ."

Then a steel portal gave way and with a roar they burst into the sky high over Tokyo.

Chapter 4

They were plummeting into the shadow circle in the center of Tokyo. "Don't just sit there screaming!" Fieh Chan said. "This is a two-pilot machine. I'm not in a fit state to handle it by myself."

"I'm not screaming!" she screamed, and then sullenly took hold of the lever he indicated. "We're going to crash into . . ."

The skyscraper loomed up alongside the Takashimaya department store, with its gaudy pennant logo streaming in the wind. Instinctively she ducked. Overhead, the curve of the Mother Ship dominated the skyline, brooding. They were going to smash right into the building. She could see the skywalk and the mannequins in the window dressed in the latest Kenzo fashions, when suddenly—

They soared skyward! And careened sideways, flip-flopping around one of the skywalks, they were upside down for a moment—

Then abruptly they righted themselves.

Tomoko looked down.

Crowds: angry, jubilant, rioting. People crammed into the streets, streaming between the cars, knocking the robot traffic police from their pedestals (she'd always loved those robot police; they were just like things in a science fiction story), brakes slamming, cars caroming into one another, people jostling, bustling, pointing skyward, and as the shuttlecraft threaded the narrow canyon between two glass-fronted skyscrapers, she followed the direction of their pointing and saw—

The sky blanketed with red! And she saw the Mother Ship that had cast its grim, awesome shadow over the streets of the metropolis slowly, slowly easing out of its resting place, turning, aiming itself at the crimson-stained clouds.

"It's happening at last," she said. "We're free, we're free of you at last!"

"Take the controls." Fieh Chan was coughing and his eyes seemed bloodshot. "I think . . . I think there's a leak in the ventilation system, I think the red dust might have . . ."

They were diving. They were going to crash! Squeezing her eyes shut, she rammed her fists down on the console, hoping, praying. They zoomed upward. "That's it. Steer us far above the toxin layer," he said, breathing uneasily.

They were way up now. She saw the dust spreading beneath them like a coiling pool of blood. Fieh Chan was breathing in slow, uneven gasps. "I'll die unless . . . I seal myself into the pressure skin. . . . Back of the shuttlecraft. . . ." He crawled to the rear of the vehicle, drew a plastic packet out of a bin. "Just don't let us lose any more altitude!" he rasped in his reptile voice, and she held the controls steady, one eye firmly on what she thought was an altimeter, though its markings were in a script—or some kind of hieroglyphics—that she couldn't understand. Fieh Chan squirmed his way forward to the front of the craft.

Tomoko Jones would never forget what she saw next.

Starting at the edges of his face, he slid his fingers under the skin and began carefully to peel down his human mask. Glistening, slimy reptile scales appeared beneath the skin. They were mottled, a dozen shades of green. He started to rend away the mask now. She'd never forget the crack of ripping dermoplast, the mucuslike effluvium that welled up between the scales. He continued, shedding his human clothes and casting them to the floor of the shuttlecraft. The skin of his neck, his chest, the curved claws peering through ridged flesh; they were as sharp as the throwing stars Matt used to scare her with around the house. The strangely abrupt joints of his alien musculature—he was bony and soft in all the wrong places, she thought. A monster out of her childhood nightmares, yet, in some terrible fashion, beautiful too.

Quickly he threw the contents of the plastic packet over himself. It seethed as it bonded to his skin. "Nothing as big as a bacterium can get through this molecular shielding device," he said, "but it will still admit oxygen. It's my own invention, a prototype. Not that many exist. Now is the time to test it on myself. Now, quick. Take us out past Tokyo, past Yokohama bay, out into open country. It'll be easier there. I'm sealed in now."

"But the altimeter," she protested as the gauge she had been watching began to dip dangerously, though she didn't think they had changed altitude.

"That's no altimeter! That's the fuel gauge!" Fieh Chan shouted in alarm. "Ten more minutes and we're gone!"

"What do you want me to do?"

"On my signal, press that button!"

He positioned himself for something, his tongue flicking back and forth in feverish excitement.

"Now!"

"But what about me?"

"There's a parachute in the back!"

"But I've never—"

"Push the button!"

Now!

She banged down with all her might. Suddenly the floor beneath them trembled and the seat Fieh Chan had been occupying buckled under and she heard and felt a turbulent rush of air—

He was gone!

Where was he?

Suddenly she caught sight of him sailing earthward, the red and blue silk of a parachute streaming from his back, his eyes closed in some inscrutable emotion. The parachute opened now. He plunged down into the scarlet cloud layer below. Would the pressure skin be enough to prevent him from dying horribly, being eaten alive from within? As she watched him, she wondered why she was feeling such sympathy for him, a creature who had probably eaten human flesh, who had come to this planet for the express purpose of subjugating and enslaving its people. For ever and ever he seemed to fall, and at last the dust cloud swallowed him. She couldn't tell if he was dead or alive.

But somehow she knew she hadn't seen the last of him.

Only minutes left. The craft was veering back toward the city, out of control. The fuel gauge read zero—that much at least she could tell! The shuttle was rocking in the turbulent air. She crawled into the back, fumbled for what might be the parachute—

There, was that it? She'd never seen one up close; she'd only watched people put them on in newsreels and in adventure movies. No time to think now! She strapped herself in and went back to the front. She knotted her *yukata* firmly about her waist, worrying suddenly about modesty, and stood in the position she'd seen Fieh Chan in . . . then she slammed her hand down on the button he'd told her to push, and—

Panic! She was in the air! The wind battering her! And the shuttlecraft, pilotless, sailing on. She watched it plummet out of sight, saw a flash of light, far off, through the red mist of the dust cloud.

Then she pulled the cord.

For a moment nothing happened, and she thought, *Jesus God, this isn't even a parachute, it's some alien device that has nothing to do with parachuting, for all I know it's an article of lizard clothing or*—

And it opened!

Slowly, so slowly, she began her descent . . .

Brilliant blue of the tiled roofs, eaves upturned . . .
dayglo-lime-colored paddy fields full of young rice, and
the wind wafting her toward the jagged skyline of Tokyo in
the distance.

My life! she thought.

Scenes flashed through her head:

She was a little girl and her parents were fighting and her
mother was saying, "We have to teach her some of the old
ways; she has to grow up knowing who she is," and her
father furiously saying, "This is America, Sachiko, and I
don't want you speaking that heathen language in my
house," and Mom said, "Then why did you marry me?"
and so on and so on into the night while little Tomoko cried
herself to sleep clutching a brown-furred girl teddy bear in a
kimono—

Watching Matt, admiring his sweat-beaded torso as he
ran in the park, she a college girl buried in her anthropology
books, picking the same bench day in and day out to watch
him running by, not having the courage to stop him to ask
his name until one day he skidded to a halt like a well-oiled
machine and smiled at her and he said, "No, I don't even go
to school here; I'm just working out for the tournament
three months from now," and eventually they'd made love
and were married and she'd clung to him desperately,
needing to escape her old home and find her true identity,
but somehow it had all gone sour—

The ground beneath! It was too near; she was going too
fast. *I'm going to die!* she thought, and felt herself slipping
into unconsciousness.

Chapter 5

Someone was prodding her. . . . She stirred. Opened her eyes. A kid and an old man recoiled.

"Ee! Bijitaa daroo!" the old man said, covering the boy's eyes and making him scramble out of the way. Mud on her face, her arms; bruises everywhere. *Thank God I didn't land on the road!* she thought, looking up and seeing the pavement only a few yards away. A paddy field had broken her fall; six inches of muddy water, a sheet of soft young rice.

But what was the man saying?

"Bijitaa da! Bijitaa!" the child was shrieking, pointing at her, obviously in a wild panic.

What was this word *bijitaa, bijitaa*? Oh, she remembered now. That was how they pronounced the word *visitor* in the Japanese language. They thought she was one of *them*! She looked about wildly. The parachute was spread out over the rice. Over the bright orange silk was the unmistakable insignia of the Visitors. Quickly she unstrapped herself, struggled to get up.

In her halting Japanese, trying to use the most polite level possible, she said, *"Bijitaa ja nai desu. . . . Hito, hito de gozaimasu."* Please, I'm not a Visitor. I'm human, human. Oh, please. Her throat felt so terribly parched. "Do you have water? Water? *O-mizu o o-negai shimasu?"* Damn,

she couldn't tell if she'd gotten it right. The old man and the
boy stared curiously at her and at each other.

"I'm American," she went on in slow Japanese. "I need
to get to Tokyo. I'm not a Visitor."

"Madam," said the old man, "it is clear you are not one.
You have not succumbed to the red dust."

Water on her face . . . a gentle drizzle . . . the
raindrops looked like blood, for they had formed around
particles of the toxin scattered in the atmosphere.

"Are we truly free now?" she whispered. "Truly?"

The old man said, "An alien craft crashed about two
kilometers from here. Two parachutes were seen."

"Where is the other one?" Tomoko said, remembering
how Fieh Chan had looked as he fell, his look of almost
Zen-like peace. Was he dead already? Somehow she knew
that he wasn't. There was something remarkable about that
reptile commander.

"The other parachute has not been traced. If it was a
Bijitaa, it has doubtless perished."

"Please help me. I have to go to Tokyo. I have to go
home!"

Presently the two strangers, convinced that she was not
an alien, took her to a small house on the other side of the
paddy field and gave her water. The wind had carried her
fairly far out of the city. It had seemed such a tiny distance
from high up in the sky, but now it seemed insurmountable.
But she couldn't stay. Thanking her helpers profusely, she
staggered over to the side of the road. She walked a couple
of kilometers, found a phone booth, and realized that she
had, of course, no money. She didn't know whether it was
acceptable to hitchhike. After spending all those months in
an Ainu village, she wasn't all that acquainted with how the
"civilized" people lived. *I'll have to try it,* she thought in
desperation, and stood in the shoulder sticking out her
thumb. Surely they'd seen enough Hollywood movies to
understand that hand signal! Not many cars came by; most
were going away from the city. She decided to keep

walking . . . by nightfall she'd reached the outer suburbs. A side street; a sign leading to the labyrinthine Tokyo subway system.

But I don't have any money! she told herself again. However, people were rushing past, ignoring the ticket-vending machines. She rode the escalator down to the lower level and discovered that there was no one collecting tickets. She stood dubiously for a moment, and then someone shouted at her to go through. "*Kyo wa saabisu,*" she heard him say.

"Today it's free?"

"No one cares today. Today we celebrate!"

She merged with the stream of people; she had to wait almost an hour for a train. They must not be running regularly today. *Where am I going?* she thought as she waited, remembering suddenly that she was still only dressed in a muddy *yukata* and that it was only the extreme politeness of these people that prevented them from staring or commenting.

There was a festive mood on the train. People were actually passing around bottles of sake and toasting each other, embracing each other in tears. It must be true after all—they must really be liberated. By the time they pulled into Meguro station, she was feeling properly drunk and singing along with them, even though she didn't know the words of any of the songs.

As she emerged into the neon-bright night, she saw crowds thronging in the pachinko arcades. Vendors were hawking noodles and skewers of chicken in the streets. No one was paying for anything. You could hardly get through the alleys, they were so congested. Here and there were tremendous bonfires where they were burning lizards in effigy and people danced wildly about.

She turned down a little lane that led into the Kamiosaki sector. She was making her way to the Tokyo office of the anthropology exchange program she had been involved with.

She found it, knocked on the door, was let in by a night watchman, who was clearly high on life and booze, was ushered her into a little hallway, and—

"Mein Gott!" A squeaky tenor voice said from the top of the staircase. She recognized it instantly. "We thought you were dead. You've been gone for months."

"Dr. Schwabauer!" At last, someone she knew. She started weeping with relief. "My God, I thought you might still be on the ship, in that terrible terrible food locker."

The professor hobbled down the stairs. She looked at him; he beamed and came to give her a hug.

"Professor, this sounds weird, but I've never seen you without a tie before!" she said. It was silly, but she couldn't think of anything else to say.

He was a lanky man, bald, wearing a pair of wire-rimmed spectacles. He'd always been so fastidious—anal-retentive she used to call him—but today he actually had his shirt on inside out. "I thought you were dead, I was sure you were," she said.

"No, the German consulate bargained for my release," he replied. "But as for the Ainu village, well, nobody much seems to give a damn about the Ainu. No one but a few anthropologists. And you, Tomoko, I had long given you up for dead. The Americans haven't had any luck getting their people out of the Visitor strongholds here because of reprisals against the resistance movement in the States. They freed you anyway, though?"

"Oh, Professor, I've had such a narrow escape! I almost died. I woke up hanging in some kind of amniotic sack, and they took me to see Fieh Chan, and they wanted me to make love to him or they were going to have me for dinner."

"You saw Fieh Chan himself?" Dr. Schwabauer said. "According to the latest news reports, he is presumed dead. They've no proof, but apparently the toxin renders the bodies pretty much unrecognizable. The Visitor mission on the Ginza is in flames." He looked at her gravely. "But you haven't even eaten, have you?"

"Nothing but saline solution or whatever they pumped into me for months on end. Has it really been that long?"

"Yes. But it's all over now." The sounds of the crowd came bursting in from outside, shouts and cheering and the thunder of thousands of feet in the square outside Meguro station. "It's all over."

"I can hardly believe it." And deep inside she couldn't believe it. There was something not quite right, something missing. *Call it intuition, call it whatever,* she thought, *but I can't believe they've gone for good.*

"Relax. Soon you will be going home."

Home, she thought. It seemed infinitely far away, that sunny house in southern California and her handsome husband and the freeways and the Jacuzzis and the idle chatter of the neighbors. "Home, home, home," she said. She couldn't stop weeping.

Later she lay down to sleep in a European-style bed under an electric fan. She could hear the professor tapping away at his typewriter from a room next door. It was a familiar sound, one she'd heard every single day of their fieldwork. She used to try to count the rat-tat-tats; it was her way of getting to sleep. But in spite of the exhaustion of the day's events—she was sure she'd lived through more than one lifetime in a single day, that day—she couldn't get to sleep for a long time. She kept seeing visions of southern California.

To go home. It was what she longed for. Wasn't it?

But now and then the image of the alien's face would steal into her consciousness.

"He's dead," she said aloud, trying to force the fact on herself. "They said so on the news, didn't they?"

But she would remember that she had been about to kiss him, to make love to him—and that she had felt no revulsion at all.

PART TWO

CALIFORNIA: FOUR MONTHS LATER

Chapter 6

Haataja, California: a tiny township sticking out of one end of Santa Ana, a few minutes down the freeway from Disneyland. An eminent Finnish émigré had given his name to the town, as a result of which no one could pronounce it. Almost as though in compensation for this, its streets had some of the most whitebread names in southern California. They were all called Spruce and Maple and Walnut. It was at the triune intersection of those particular streets that the one shopping plaza in town was to be found. Once it had been a favorite hanging-out spot for the local teenagers, but ever since the opening of Orange Mall down the road, it had tended to be rather deserted. Only a couple of places in it still did good business. One was Po Sam's Diner,—American and Chinese cuisine, whose food was as splendid as its decor was dingy. The other was the Matt Jones Institute of Martial Arts.

Late afternoon: in the lull before the adult evening classes, Matt Jones strolled across the plaza into Po Sam's.

"Hey!" he said, easing himself onto a counter stool. "What's for dinner, Sam?"

The man at the wok said, "Lizard stew, Matt! Wanna taste?"

"What? Still on lizard jokes after four months?" Matt sighed. He looked around. A projection TV, overhead, blared forth a beer commercial. In the corner a twelve-year-old kid was purposefully banging away on a video game. It was a scene of idyllic suburban bliss. It was hard to imagine that only a few short months ago they'd lived in utter terror of being captured by Visitors and herded onto the ships as slaves—or food. "Just make me anything you want," he said to Sam.

"Lizard lo mein? Lizard à la king?"

"Yeah, whatever."

He turned to watch the kid on the video game. In between screens, the boy waved and said, "Hi, Matt."

Matt replied, "Hi, CB. Done your homework?"

"Hey, don't talk to me, dude. I'm checking something out on this 'Galaga' game."

"What?" But the kid had gone back to the game.

He's really a lot better than he was a year ago, Matt thought. He cast his mind back, as he so often did, to the day he had first met the boy. How could he ever forget that day? It was the day Tomoko had walked out on him.

She had just stalked away. He stood dumbly staring after her. Nothing like this had ever happened to him before. "If that's what you want," he hollered, "fine!" The plaza was pretty much empty, but some of the regulars from Po Sam's had turned to stare. "Get out of my life. Go to goddamn Japan or wherever it is, I don't care!"

Then he'd gone back into the martial arts school and slammed the door of his office.

A little kid looked up at him: nicely dressed, very WASP, blond hair and blue eyes. At the moment, sheepish.

"Who the hell are you?"

"Er, my name's Chris Baer, sir. My friends call me CB. I'm registering for k-k-karate class?"

"Sorry I took out my stuff on you."

"Your wife just left you?" said the kid with the appalling tactlessness of childhood. "I understand," he went on. "My 'rents just got a divorce. We used to live in the Valley. Made me feel like shit."

He didn't know what to say, whether to get angry or cry. He just stared at the kid like a department store dummy, and then broke out laughing. It was just so awful, he couldn't stop.

A few months after that the Visitors came.

One evening, after closing time, he went back to his office to get something and heard someone sniffling in there. A burglar? Rodents? He turned on the light. The kid was sitting all scrunched up in the big office chair. He'd obviously been crying his guts out. "Hey," Matt said softly, "what's wrong?"

CB said, "I didn't have anywhere left to go—nowhere."

"Okay, tell me about it. I mean, you were there when I had *my* crisis, right? So I owe you a favor." And he sat the kid down on the sofa, fixed him a cup of hot chocolate, and listened. In the back of his mind he wondered what Tomoko would have made of this. Tomoko was always telling him how narcissistically macho he was, how he'd sooner stand around flexing his muscles than listen to anyone's problems. Was it the fact that she was gone that was making him take greater care not to tread on people's egos? He tried not to think about her at all and turned his attention to CB's story.

"They're dead," CB said. "They're history, they're like totally dead."

"Relax. Who's dead?"

"My goddamn 'rents, that's who! I didn't have anywhere to go. I just hitched a ride here."

"You shouldn't have done that. You never know—"

"Why should I be scared of people? I mean we got man-eating lizards hanging over our heads. I saw them—I saw them—I'm gonna kill them!"

"It's all right." Diffidently he patted the boy on the shoulder. He wasn't a very affectionate person, and it made him feel awkward. The kid was shaking something fierce.

"Well, we went back to our old neighborhood, see? My mom and I. I mean, to see Dad. I mean, they thought they might get together again. I saw this kid I used to know real well, Sean Donovan? His dad's a TV journalist. We used to be on the same little league team, but, like, he's all *weird* now. He didn't talk about baseball or nothing, he just kept telling me what cool dudes the Visitors are. He was on board their Mother Ship! Some other guy told me they'd kept Sean in a meat locker and ran him through some c-c-conversion chamber and that's what made him turn out weird."

"Donovan, Donovan. . . . Yeah, didn't he have something to do with that exposé, showing how the Visitors are really reptiles? A lot of people still don't believe that."

"I saw it, man! I found out my dad was in the resistance. They came and raided our old house. I hid in the hall closet, there's this top shelf you can't see that well where I kept all my action figures, and there's like this knothole you can look out of and see the living room. I saw them come down the street in their uniforms and their guns. They were banging on the door and Dad said, 'Don't go, Judy, don't go. I think it's *them*,' but it was too late, she'd already opened the door and was standing there just being nice, just you know smiling at them, and then this tall Visitor, I saw it through the hole, man, this Visitor, he reaches out and grabs her and *throws* her across the hall and she slams against the wall, and I see that her neck's on wrong, it's dangling at an angle, I know it can't be happening. Then they started laughing and laughing and one of them grabbed my dad and held him still and forced him to watch while they . . . they . . . oh, Jesus, they . . . they ate my mother!"

"Christ."

"Then they killed my dad. Clubbed him on the head with one of those laser rifles. But before he died, he grabbed the face of the one that was holding on to him, you know, and it came off in his hand. I mean the face tore off like one of those special-effects masks. It was all rubbery and gooey and slimy, and underneath it were scales, snake scales, and his eyes were . . . his eyes . . . Oh, I'm scared, Mr.

Jones, I got nowhere to go, you're the only grown-up I know around here."

Matt had always been a loner; things rarely touched him. But he had to help. Not only because they were both human beings and the enemy was an alien . . . but also because he suddenly realized that the kid would fulfill a need he never knew had before. "God," he said, never thinking he would ever say it aloud, "God, I miss my wife. I wish she hadn't gone away. I wish she'd have stayed and we could have had a baby and . . . but how could I wish such a terrible thing? How could I wish to bring new life into this world, knowing that the rulers are . . . evil, horrifying reptiles?" But there was a gaping void in his life. Oh, it wasn't sex . . . he could get that anytime, looking the way he did—there was no use pretending he wasn't attractive to women—and playing all those state and national tournaments. It was something else.

He said, "Look, kid, what're you going to do?"

"How should I know?"

"You can't go home."

"I got relatives in Tempe, Arizona. The Karneys."

"How're you going to get there?"

"I know where Mom kept her petty cash."

"But—" Matt knew what he was going to say; he could have sworn the kid knew too. "Look, I . . . I got a big house here in Haataja. I got a pool. I got . . . I mean, I live alone."

CB smiled wanly. "Hey, thanks, dude."

That was how CB had come to live at Matt's house. And Matt had started to teach him—not just the stuff they taught in the martial arts school, but the secrets he had learned from his master. Not just the standard moves people see on TV. Most people who signed up for the course, they were women who wanted to fend off rapists (though sometimes you'd wonder what these particular women had to worry about) or guys who wanted to impress their friends. He'd never have thought to teach them any *real* martial arts. But

CB was so anxious to learn. He was afflicted with a profound melancholy; only working out again and again seemed to drive the demons from his small, lithe body. He seemed to have a fantasy about combating the Visitors somehow, about singlehandedly destroying them. And he adored Matt; he thought of them as a team, like Batman and Robin.

Theirs was a strange family, thrown together from necessity; but somehow they got along.

"Your kid much, much better now," Sam said, plunking a vast plate of steaming noodles and meat on the table.

"What is this?" Matt said.

"Lizard ho fan," Sam said. "Giant rice noodles with diced Visitor."

"Oh, come on!" said Matt, deftly manipulating his chopsticks. It was so delicious he decided not to ask Sam what it was.

"But seriously, your kid much better. I remember first time he came here. Very sad, always crying. Now happy, play video games."

"Yeah," Matt said, regarding his adoptee with pride. "I was just thinking about how we met."

There was a long lull; CB was just standing there, not firing, and Matt couldn't hear the usual beeping noises that the "Galaga" machine always emitted. "Need a quarter?" he said, fumbling in his pocket.

"No. I just learned this great way to beat the machine."

"What do you mean?" Matt said, going over to the video game and looking over the boy's shoulder. Two of the enemy ships were left, and CB's ship had retreated into one corner and wasn't firing at all.

"My friend Mia Alvarez told me about it. You see, like on the first screen, you know, you kill everything but the two bees on the farthest left. Then you wait down in this corner for ten minutes, not firing or nothing. You just wait."

"For ten minutes?" Matt said. "That's hard to believe."

"No. I don't know how it works. It's something to do with the algorithm used to figure out the number of enemy bullets, but—"

"You've lost me," said Matt, who, like many adults in his age group, didn't really understand computerese too well.

"Okay. Now watch." The two enemy starships that were left had slowed their fire now . . . in a couple of minutes they were only firing one bullet each . . . now they were firing none. "Time for action," CB said. Then he wasted the two enemy ships, and the screen started to fill with more . . . and then the starships started swooping down, but . . . they didn't fire! "See?" said CB, firing madly with his forefinger and making his ship dart back and forth frantically. "If you follow all these steps, it disables the enemy fire completely. They never fire again, and you can go on and on and never get shot at, never lose a guy unless one crashes into you, and you can like turn it over three, four times before you get too tired. I got four million points yesterday."

"What about your homework?" said Matt, who hated to play the heavy.

"Homework—I did it already. But you know something? When I'm lurking in that corner, waiting out those ten minutes, I imagine what I'm going to do to *them*. I mean, the lizards."

"They're gone now."

"But that's how to win against them maybe—just keep dodging their fire until they think we're just too chicken to fight back anymore. Then they'll be fooled into thinking we're wimps, they won't even bother to shoot us anymore, and then—"

"We strike!"

"Awesome!" the kid said as he penetrated the fourteenth level without losing a single ship.

"Well, that's fine, CB. As long as you can get some—ahem—real-life lesson from that video game." But the kid was in a trance now, his mind on the revenge he was going to exact from the reptiles from the stars.

At that moment, Sam called him. "Hey, your food getting cold!" Matt returned to the counter. The news was on the projection TV, and he glanced up at it—

"This is Ace Crispin for Orange County Evening News. Godzilla movies are the subject of controversy in Tokyo, Japan, today as—"

At the mention of Japan he started to pay attention. There were a few views of pagodas and skyscrapers, then a scene from some movie where a giant reptile was stomping all over Tokyo.

Voice-over: *"The provisional post-Visitor government passed an official ban on the showing of seven different types of monster movies. Experts on the island nation are baffled. The Japanese government's new minister of culture, Mr. Ogawa, stated—"*

Image of an elderly Japanese man in a business suit addressing a grave assembly of formally attired men and kimono-clad women.

" 'We consider it improper at this time to present any antireptile propaganda that might reflect badly on the image of our former Bijitaa rulers, who have temporarily retired into outer space. We feel that the people of Japan should not get into an erroneous frame of mind regarding reptiles during the interregnum.' Mr. Ogawa was appointed to the Japanese cabinet during the period of Visitor domination—"

"My God!" Matt said. "Does that mean . . . does this mean it could happen again?"

Sam nodded sagely. "Happen already, that's what I think."

"But the red dust, the toxin . . . aren't they all dead?"

"Who knows?" said Sam, never pausing as he peeled a mountain of shrimp and threw them one by one into a pot. "Lizard come once, lizard can come again."

Matt thought of Tomoko. He'd tried so long not to think about her, but . . . she was out there somewhere! And if, somehow, the nightmare was beginning all over again in Tokyo, maybe she was in danger, maybe she was already dead. . . .

He munched listlessly on Sam's food. CB was still playing "Galaga," whooping with glee whenever he turned it over. He thought of how CB had found out how to cheat at the game. *How do people ever learn these things?* he thought. *And when one finds out, pretty soon every kid in the world seems to know it.* He thought of how the kid had compared his way of playing the game with the humans' fight for freedom. But maybe it was the aliens who were like CB's ship—waiting, quietly waiting for the moment when the earthlings had exhausted their ammunition and they could slip back and reconquer the world. He shuddered.

Someone walked into the restaurant. It was Anne Williams, his secretary. She was also the school's official specialist in *wu shih*, the variety of kung fu where you imitate the actions of five real and mythical beasts. She was wearing a headband and black leather spiked suspenders on lavender parachute pants. (Sexy, he thought.)

"Here, Matt. A telegram for you. Thought you might want to see it right away." She brushed back a strand of her red hair.

He tore it open. Was it from Tomoko? The international mail, disrupted since the alien takeover, had only recently started up again, he'd heard.

But no. It wasn't from her.

It wasn't from anyone he knew.

It wasn't even signed.

It said:

BEWARE
THE ALIEN SWORDMASTER
IS COMING.

Chapter 7

That evening, in the office, CB was finishing off his homework in one corner, Anne had gone home, and Matt was figuring out some tax deductions for the quarter.

"What was that telegram all about?" CB asked, looking up from his seventh grade English textbook. "The alien swordmaster . . . weird. Probably some prankster."

"It's nothing," Matt said distractedly. He didn't want to admit that he had found it disturbing.

"Any news on that tournament you and Lex Nakashima are organizing?"

"You know, that's strange. I haven't heard from Lex in over a week, and he was supposed to get back to me about something. I think I'll call."

Matt picked up the phone, used his MCI access code and dialed New York.

"No, Matt," CB said. "Three hours of jet lag, remember?"

"Yah. He ought to be at home, not at work." He hung up and redialed a number in Westchester. Lex was one of his oldest buddies; they'd been pitted against each other countless times in their youth, and both had achieved national ranking in several martial arts disciplines. In fact, Lex was, Matt had to admit, just a tad better than him at it . . . although Matt knew better than to feel envy.

"Hi . . . sorry to bother you so late, but. . . ." he began.

He heard a woman sobbing on the other end.

"Crystal, is that you?" he said. "What's the matter?"

"He's gone, he's upped and gone!"

"Uh oh," CB said, seeing the expression on Matt's face. "Trouble, huh?"

"Shush, CB. What do you mean, Lex is gone? We got the tournament to work out, and—"

Crystal's voice started to sound hysterical. "He didn't come home last night. I just went out to the grocery store and . . . bloodstains on the bedsheets, I called the police, they said there was evidence of a struggle, and . . ."

"Oh, no!" He motioned to CB to come closer so he could hear. "Was anything suspicious happening at the time? I mean, did he get in a fight with someone?" Lex loved to brawl.

"Nothing. Oh, the usual, you know how he is. But . . . oh, and we got a crank telegram two days ago."

"What did it say?" Matt asked, but he already knew what her reply would be.

"It said, 'Beware, the alien swordmaster is coming.' I mean, just a harmless prank probably, you know how those kids are, dressing up as ninjas and terrorizing the neighborhood and such."

"For Christ's sake, Crystal, don't stay at home tonight!"

"What do you think—"

"Go to a friend's house. Go to the police. I think . . . I think something pretty fishy is going on."

"OK, Matt. My god, do you think he's—"

"I don't know!" Matt said. "Just be careful. *Be careful!*" He hung up. He said to CB: "I think we'd better get outa town, kiddo. I don't think this is some prank. Maybe someone's trying to fix the tournament."

"But Matt, like it's not supposed to be a competition, really . . . just a demonstration of all you guys' skills and stuff, right? And TV cameras, maybe a documentary or something.''

"You never know," Matt said. "Come on, let's go home and pack.''

"Does this mean I don't have to finish my homework?" CB said, brightening up.

"Certainly not! You will take your textbooks with you, young man.''

"Grody.''

"OK. Help me lock up the place now, all right?''

A half hour later they were done at the office. It was dark. They always walked home; it was only about a mile. Matt didn't have an ounce of fat on him, and he intended to keep it that way.

The way home: down Spruce a couple of blocks, then, cleverly dodging down an alleyway that kind of sneaked up on you, in between two fast-food joints, and you were suddenly under the freeway; then through a patch of woods and there you were in pure suburbia.

They stopped for a hamburger before they darted into the alley.

"So what do you think?" CB said.

"About what?''

"You know.''

"I . . . I don't know what to think. Hey, what did you think of that news item about banning Godzilla movies in Japan?" Trying to change the subject.

"Dumbest thing I ever heard of. I used to think giant lizards were, hey, cool, you know, like they could knock down those awesome buildings but you could see the whole time they were just dudes in lizard suits. Then I ran into lizards in human suits . . . guess I don't think Godzilla's that rad anymore. Hey, you think that. . . .''

"Yeah.''

They turned into the alley.

"What the—" Pain thudded into his cranium. He spun around and saw a human shape coiling back into the shadow . . . a man dressed as a ninja. "CB!" he shouted. A second ninja was climbing down the wall. CB whirled around, leaped up and kicked him in the groin before double-somersaulting in the air and landing on his feet. A metallic cry escaped the ninja's throat.

"The other one!" the boy shrieked.

Matt's arm lashed out. The ninja ducked deftly and seemed to blend with the darkness. "No you don't!" CB cried and rammed into him like a hitter sliding into home plate. The ninja grunted, tried to get up.

"These aren't real ninjas!" Matt said. "They don't know a damn thing about it, they're about as elegant as elephants. They're amateurs, they're just dressing up. Let's give it to them, Robin!"

"Hey, Batman!" the kid shouted, and dodged abruptly as the second one pounced at him like a tiger. He slammed into the wall. CB rushed him, started to hit him again and again, his small tense hands knifing the air.

"Hey, cool it . . . no anger," Matt said. "Be cool inside. Like an iceberg."

CB was breathing heavily; the ninja slumped to the ground. "Where'd the other guy go?"

"I think he split."

"Don't be too sure."

"Guess not."

Suddenly he sprang down from overhead, catlike—

"Yaaaa!" Matt shouted, keeping his body perfectly still as he sent all his strength exploding into his arms, bursting through his fingertips with volcanic force—the ninja toppled on top of the one on the pavement, just as he'd managed to heave himself up to start crawling away.

The one who had jumped them ran off into the night.

They looked at each other, then at the one at their feet.

"Good work," Matt said.

"I think we ought to call the cops," CB said. "I mean, is it safe to go home?"

"Wait a minute! Look at him!"

Matt knelt down. There was an odd fizzing sound, like gas escaping from a balloon. CB said, "What's that noise? Is he dead?"

"Dunno."

Matt stared to pull away the mask from the ninja's face . . . that wheezing sound again . . . something clear, a plastic membrane or something, came loose in his hands. It smelled sweet, like amyl acetate.

They looked at their attacker's face. It was an Asian face, a young man. Matt yanked away at the membranous sheath; it tore with a harsh sound, like velcro, and more air seemed to gush forth from it.

Then, as they watched, their assailant's eyes opened wide. He cried out: "No . . . not the molecular pressure skin . . . my only protection . . ." And he started to scream horribly.

Then his face began to melt and char. Matt covered the kid's eyes. He didn't want to look himself. But he couldn't help it. He saw the skin peel away, saw the glistening green scales beneath, saw the stone-cold topaz-colored eyes, saw the lizard-man writhe in anguish as his very flesh burned up. . . .

"Let me look, Matt! I wanna see him, they killed my Mom and Dad—" the kid squealed.

"No. No, kid." The kid tore Matt's hand away from his eyes and stared, just stared, his face a mask of terrible anger.

"Come on. We gotta get back. We probably ought to get out of town."

"I wanna fight! I wanna kill them!"

"Don't . . . don't, CB. Come on, kid."

He looked one last time at the sizzling, melting thing that had once been alive. The piece of clear plastic-like stuff he'd pulled off the creature's face was drifting in the night breeze. He bent down to pick it up. It might be useful to someone . . . someone in the resistance. If the resistance was still around. If they hadn't been lulled into packing away their ammunition, like the starships in that video game.

Slowly they walked back to the house.

A lot later that night. . . .

Matt couldn't sleep after what he'd seen. He tossed and turned.

CB dreamed about the night the Visitors had come to the house in the Valley. He woke up. Every time he closed his eyes again he'd see them. He'd see their eyes. He'd see the blood dripping from their fanged mouths. He'd see his mother lying headless on their living room carpet. He'd wake up. Screaming.

A slim figure stood in the door of Matt's bedroom.

"Can I come in?"

"Sure."

"I'm sorry, but—"

"Why aren't you asleep?"

"I can't help it, Matt! When you covered my eyes, I just had to look anyway, I *had* to! You understand?"

"I understand." He beckoned the boy into the room. CB sat down on the side of the bed. "Lizard ninjas! Is nothing sacred?" he said, trying to coax a laugh out of the kid. But CB just sat there solemnly.

At last he said, "Look, I know it's not exactly cool, I mean, like I *am* twelve years old, but . . ."

Matt waited.

"I just don't think I can be alone right now. I mean, OK, don't get mad already, but—"

Matt laughed. "We'll lick 'em. You and me."

"Thanks. Thanks . . . thanks, Dad."

"You've never called me Dad before," Matt said, strangely moved. He laid his hand on the boy's sweat-drenched forehead.

CB stirred, sighed, breathed deeply, and fell asleep.

V

But Matt couldn't sleep. He stayed up until dawn, his mind playing and replaying everything that had happened that day, trying to make some sense out of it. At last, as the sun rose, he fell into an uneasy sleep for an hour or two. When he woke up again he saw that CB hadn't moved from where he'd fallen asleep at the edge of the bed.

Maybe I dreamed the whole thing, he thought.

Then his gaze wandered to the corner of the room, and he saw the tattered piece of that membrane he'd pulled off the corpse of the lizard-man, flapping against the vents of the air conditioner, and he knew it was all true, all too true.

"School," Matt whispered, from habit more than anything.

But the kid didn't stir, and Matt realized that there'd be no school that day. He wondered if life was ever going to be normal for the two of them again.

Chapter 8

Anne looked up from her desk. "Where've you been all day? I had to send in a substitute for the morning advanced—"

She looked out the window and saw Matt's Corvette. "You *drove* to work? You haven't done that in years! And," she said as CB came in behind Matt, "why isn't the kid in school? Don't tell me—it's a holiday or something. You guys look pretty disheveled, you go to bed with your clothes on? Have you been corrupting the kid again, Matthew Jones?"

Matt didn't say a word, but went right through into his own office; CB followed him, looking like a ghost.

Matt heard Anne go on, "Well, if you're not going to tell me . . . what's a secretary for? You got about six million calls. Mrs. Mayhew wants to know if her sons Joe and Bill will be back each afternoon in time for the rehearsal of their school play, they're doing *The Boys from Syracuse* down at Haataja High, and Mary Lou wants to know why you stood her up last week, and—"

"Close up the school," Matt shouted back.

"What? Oh, a joke. Well, there's about six calls from the principal of St. Rita's School. They want to know what you've been teaching these kids who've been beating up on the nuns."

"What the hell—" Matt couldn't help laughing in spite of

49

the terrible things that happened the previous evening. "Beating up nuns?"

"Oh, apparently Sister Rose has been shooting her mouth off again."

"Jesus," Matt said, coming back into the front office and throwing his hands up in the air, "the things I have to contend with when there's about to be another invasion or something!"

"Invasion?" Anne said. "Don't tell me they're going to do another drug bust in the kids' lockers again."

"No, no, invasion, as in Visitors!"

A stunned silence. Matt saw CB walk silently over to the sofa in the private office and sit down. The boy seemed remarkably calm—too calm. It was hard for Matt to admit his fear to himself, but. . . .

In the pause, the phone started to ring again.

Instinctively, Anne pushed the button and said, "Matt Jones Institute, may I help you?" She waited, drumming her fingers on the side of the desk. "Oh, hi, Rod. Matt, it's Rod Casilli."

Matt said, "I guess I'd better take it. But listen. I want you to close up the Institute, all right? I don't know what you're going to tell them—"

"What about the Junior Dragons? They're milling around at Po Sam's, waiting for their weekly workout. You know how rowdy they are. Sam's about to have a heart attack."

"Go . . . go and buy them ice cream and send them home."

"But you're always giving them the spiel about not eating too many sweets and not messing up their bodies and, you know, the body is the temple of the soul and all that—"

"Look, just this once. Believe me, it's an emergency."

"You're the boss."

"I'll say."

Sighing, Anne pulled a cash box from the safe. She extracted a twenty-dollar bill, uncreased it, folded it with the precision of an origami master, and stuck it into her headband (which bore the insignia of the Institute, a dragon swallowing the sun) so that it looked like a green feather. Then she went out.

Matt went into the private office and picked up the phone.

"It's about time, you jackass," said the gruff voice on the other end.

"Rod! How're you doing, old buddy? Haven't heard from you in a year. Are you going to appear at my big event?" Rod Casilli was the world's greatest expert at the almost totally vanished art of *ikakujitsu*, which derived its moves and holds from the leaping and ramming of an imaginary unicorn. Rod rarely appeared in public, and Matt had been trying to get him out of semiretirement for ages.

"After all those crank telegrams you've been sending me, you expect me to turn up at your exhibition? You must be mad!"

"Telegrams?" Matt said.

CB looked up. "I got a sinking feeling about this, dude," he said.

"Yeah," said Rod. "What's with this 'alien swordmaster' bullshit? Am I supposed to get all riled up and jet down to California full of rage and vengeance or something? Is this a challenge? You know I never leave home anymore."

Matt knew. Rod Casilli had bought an estate in the middle of the desert in New Mexico somewhere; no one knew exactly where it was. He knew too that in order to make this phone call, Rod would have had to drive (or jog, knowing him) twenty miles to the general store, also in the middle of nowhere. He would have to be pretty furious to do that. "Hey, calm down, Rod."

Rod spluttered.

"Hey, really, Rod," Matt said. "I didn't send you a telegram. I got one myself. So did our mutual friend Lex Nakashima—and he's vanished without a trace, according to his wife Crystal. And last night CB and I were attacked by a couple of Visitors disguised as ninjas."

"That's the most cockamamy story I've ever heard in my life," said Rod. "Everyone knows those lizards have gone back into outer space. And lizard ninjas . . . ha, ha, ha. Don't make me laugh."

"It's true!" Matt protested.

"Lizard ninjas. Did that smartass kid of yours put you up to this?"

"That kid of mine is huddling in a corner, scared to go to the bathroom, because of what happened last night."

"Don't you think this is going a little too far? I mean, April Fools' Day has come and gone."

It was useless.

They talked about trivial things for a while. Rod said, "To be serious, Matt, I really don't think I can make it. I landed this job coaching that movie star, what's-her-name, Marlene Zirkle. She's doing a TV series about an eighteenth century female kung fu fighter in England: sort of a combination martial arts–Regency romance thing. It's inane, but they're paying me enough to build an electrified fence around my entire estate. I suppose, now that those Visitors have gone, the media can go back to escapist trash again."

"They haven't gone," Matt said.

"There you go again. Hey, this actress is flying out here to train with me for a couple weeks. I'll suggest your lizard ninjas to her, we'll sell it as a series and split the money fifty-fifty, okay?"

Matt sighed and said, " 'Bye, Rod," and hung up.

Anne was standing in the doorway. "I got rid of them all. Now, would you like to tell me what's going on?"

Quickly, Matt and CB filled her in on everything that had happened.

"That's heavy," Anne said. "What are we going to do?"

"I think we should either get out of the L.A. area completely, like out to the Midwest or something. Or maybe hole up here. Turn it into a fortress."

"But why would they be after us? Their technology is

eight hundred years ahead of ours. How could they possibly *need* to capture grand masters of martial arts—and where are they taking them?"

"Who knows?" Matt said. "Okay, let's go ahead and lock up."

They made a complete round of the building; even the secret side entrance that only staff members knew about was double-locked. Matt shooed away some members of the Junior Dragons who were still waiting in the lobby of the Institute. Then they went back inside and closeted themselves in Matt's office.

Anne said, "Well, the first thing to think about is, what relationship does all this stuff have to the exhibition we're arranging?"

CB said, "Only that we've invited most of the best in the country."

"What about someone we haven't invited? Could they be in danger too?"

"You could call that guy up in Oregon who specializes in *takodo*. That's a pretty obscure school, but he's probably the best practitioner in the world at it. What's his name? Kunio Yasutake. Up in Eugene."

"Yeah," Matt said, becoming more and more confused at the implications all this might have. "Old Yasutake. I never could understand *takodo*. That's when you think yourself into the soul of an octopus, and you do everything by flinging out lines of force, like the eight arms of an octopus squeezing people to death. More akin to wrestling than to our kind of martial arts. Well, what's his number?"

"Here," she said, dialing the access code and the number off the top of her head.

"Wow! How'd you do that?" CB said. "You haven't called him in years, maybe never."

"That's what Anne does," Matt said. "When you think she's just making coffee or clearing the desk, she's actually memorizing every name and address in the National Martial Arts Association directory. Why do you think I pay her so much money? Wait. Put him on the speakerphone so we can all hear."

"I can read your mind," Anne said.

They waited tensely for someone to pick up.

They could hear a frail, aged voice: *"Moshimoshi? Yasutake desu."*

"Ah . . .my Japanese isn't that great," Anne said. "My name is Anne Williams, I work for the Matt Jones Institute—"

"Ah, Miss Wirriams! I have seen your name in National Martial Arts Association directory. How charming."

"Awesome!" said CB excitedly.

"I'm calling to ask, Mr. Yasutake—"

"No need. You are going to invite me to your tournament, no? I received telegram this morning. Such funny idea, this 'alien swordmaster.' I laugh and laugh."

"Oh—my—God," said CB.

"But, you see, I cannot come. Today I receive a personal phone call from Ogawa-san, minister of culture in Japan. He ask me to fly to Tokyo for a grand demonstration of *takodo*, first time in over four hundred years. I am deeply, deeply honored; of course, I cannot refuse."

"Put me on," Matt said. He took the reciever. "Look, Mr. Yasutake? This is Matt Jones. Yeah, I'm honored too. Look, I don't want to get into a complicated explanation, but I am so glad you're getting out of town. Please take care, for God's sake. I hope you'll be safe in Tokyo."

"Safe from whom? Alien swordmaster? Very good joke, Mr. Jones. I like jokes. Ha, ha."

He hung up.

"Well, at least they won't find him for a while," Anne said. "Who are we going to try next?"

"Wait a minute. Wait a goddamn minute!" Matt said suddenly. "Ogawa, minister of culture. Where have I heard that name before?"

"I was playing 'Galaga,' " said CB. "Yeah, of course.

The guy who banned the monster movies, don't you remember? Too much antireptile propaganda?"

"Uh-oh," they all said at the same time.

"He's one of *them*. Gotta be," CB said.

"But what about the red dust? It didn't work in Japan?" said Anne. "But I remember, on the news, footage of the Mother Ships leaving Tokyo and Peking and Seoul and Hong Kong and all those Far Eastern cities."

"Maybe this Ogawa guy is working for them," Matt said.

"But what human being in his right mind would— especially one that was a cabinet member and everything?" Anne said.

"Well, we had a lot of collaborators here too."

"He could be like Sean," CB said suddenly.

"Sean who?" said Matt.

"Don't you remember? I told you about him. He used to be one of my best friends in my old neighborhood. Sean Donovan. We always played baseball together. Then I didn't see him for a long time, like we didn't live that close anymore, and then when I went back he was like weird, totally weird. I mean, he was bragging about how he'd been inside one of them Mother Ships. He didn't even want to play catch. And his eyes were . . . like lifeless, totally lifeless. I know they did something to him. 'Cause the kid I used to know wasn't this kid. He was like cool, you know? Now all he wanted to talk about was the Visitors, about their awesome uniforms and their radical weapons. I think they can reach right into a dude's brain and just pluck out whatever it is that makes him *him*, and his best friend wouldn't even know him anymore."

Matt was chilled by how vividly the kid remembered, even after all these months. There was an awkward silence. The three stood there, staring at each other. The horror seemed to deepen. He couldn't stand it. He wanted to chop a pile of bricks with his bare hands or take on half a dozen thugs. It was terrible standing there, just waiting.

The phone rang.

They let it ring for a while.

"All right," said Anne. "Who's going to get it?"

Reluctantly Matt picked it up. "Matt Jones Institute."

"Matt—for God's sake—"

"Rod!"

"I saw them. They pulled into the estate in a black limousine. At first I thought it was Marlene Zirkle. Then I saw them get out. The sun was setting. They wore black. You could only see the slits of their eyes. I thought it was just a continuation of your practical joke, but it was just too elaborate. I slipped out the back and ran to the general store." That was why he was panting, obviously. Running twenty miles was a big deal even for someone in superb physical condition. He must have been running for a couple hours.

"Rod . . . is there a car you can borrow?"

"Yeah. Guy who owns the store'll loan me his."

"Listen, for God's sake. Drive to an airport, any airport. Catch the first plane to L.A. We'll get to the bottom of this."

"Okay. Wait. . . . Who the hell? . . . Oh, shit! They're coming into the store!"

Sounds of scuffling, of a screaming woman . . .of the phone crashing against a wall. Then the thud of fists on flesh, over and over . . . and then the phone went dead.

"Matt—" said Anne.

"I'm scared," said CB.

They heard something crash somewhere in the building, down the corridor maybe.

"I thought you locked up!" Matt yelled.

"I did," Anne whispered. "But that sounded like . . ."

"Footsteps." CB shuddered.

"I didn't hear anyone breaking in," Matt said. "You're sure you locked up?"

"As sure as I can be," Anne said. But she sounded unsure of herself. Matt didn't want to take any chances.

"Quick! Turn off the lights in the front office." CB tentatively reached his hand out beyond the door, snapped them off, and snatched his hand back. The three of them stood in a pool of light.

Footsteps.

"Let's ambush them," Matt whispered. "CB, you go behind the filing cabinet. You and I will stand on either side of the door."

"Right, boss." They obeyed instantly.

Matt flicked the last light out.

The steps came nearer, nearer—

The tension: a coiled cat waiting to pounce.

Nearer—

Someone was in the front office now, coming nearer—

"Now!" screamed Matt. His hands shot out to seize a body, a struggling body, and he felt Anne's arms wrapping themselves tightly around the person who had stepped inside. "Lights, CB!" he shouted.

The lights came on, hurting his eyes—

"Tomoko!"

He let go in a hurry.

"Just what is the meaning of this?" said the wife he hadn't seen in over a year. "I didn't know you were into all this cloak-and-dagger stuff, and . . . who's that kid?"

"Right," said Matt, turning crimson with embarrassment. "CB—Tomoko. Tomoko—CB."

CB solemnly shook her hand, his eyes wide.

"Thank God it's you," Matt said.

"Well, who else could it have been? Every entrance to the place was locked. I'm the only one you know who has a key."

"Oh . . . right. A key," Matt said sheepishly.

"Who did you think I was? An alien?"

"Well, actually . . ."

For the nth time that day they were forced to relate the whole story. It was hard for Matt to understand that she was actually back. He'd fantasized for so long about how they'd meet again, what he'd say to her. He had acted out their reunion with throbbing background music in his head and dialogue by the greatest screenwriters. He'd never expected that he'd be lying in ambush for a Visitor and instead discover *her*.

When they were through telling the story, Tomoko sat and stared at them with blank amazement.

"I spend four months trying to get home after a hair-raising escape from the Visitors . . . I come home and find out that I'm right back where I started. And someone else's kid living in my house—"

"Are you going to send me away now?" CB asked in alarm.

"The kid stays," Matt said.

"Of course he stays!" she said. And she opened arms wide to embrace them both. "Oh, Matt, you've changed. There's a new softness in you, a new compassion. I think that CB has a lot to do with it."

"We get along," Matt said.

Tomoko said, "It wasn't easy getting home, let me tell you. Things are . . . bizarre in Japan. Maybe it all has something to do with the problems you've been experiencing."

She summarized what had happened to her in the last four months. She had thought: Freedom, I'll just get on a plane and go home now. But of course things weren't that simple. The departure of the aliens had destroyed the Japanese economy. Japan had been hard hit; half Tokyo had been left in ruins before it had been subjugated, and the willingness of the people to perform *kamikaze* attacks on Visitor installations had made peacekeeping a more violent and costly process during the Visitor regime. When they went away, Japan was bereft of working postal and telephone services; she'd tried to reach Matt for months and finally had just given up. The Ministry of Culture was restricting air travel in order to avoid what they called "cultural pollution," and Tomoko had been on the waiting list for three months; Professor Schwabauer, who had sometimes used to come to dinner at their house, was still unable to leave Japan, either to return to his teaching post in America or to go to his home in Germany.

"But I'm here now," Tomoko said.

"Yes, I'm glad," Matt said. "And confused, too."

"Before I left you would never have admitted that." She kissed him lightly on the lips. There was nothing sexual in it at all. That was wonderful to him, because since she had left him, he had never just been close to a woman without intending to conquer her. Seeming to read his mind, she said, "Yes, I'm not like the other women."

"There never were—" he began.

She only smiled. And he knew she knew, and he knew she understood and forgave him.

Anne said, "Forgive me for interrupting this wonderfully mushy scene, but maybe you can tell us more about what's happening in Japan? Do you know anything about this Ogawa, their minister of culture?"

"Yes," Tomoko said. "Before Fieh Chan's . . . death, it was said that the two were intimately connected."

"And now? What's this about banning monster movies? It seems pretty silly to me," Anne said.

"Oh, they're really into cultural purity now. They've had all kinds of edicts. They want to put back the clock to the sixteenth century, before all the Europeans came along."

"You think it's a front for something else?" said CB.

"Who knows? All I know is that technology has gone down the tubes in a big way, and they have sword-carrying people in samurai costume patrolling the streets."

"Cool!" CB whispered.

"And they're always stopping people and demanding to see their papers."

"Like Nazis or something!" CB said.

"All I know is," Tomoko said, "that I'm glad to be home."

"For how long?" CB said, voicing the concern uppermost in their minds. . . .

V

* * *

That night Anne moved into the Joneses' living room. They were afraid something would happen if they didn't all stick together.

And Matt and Tomoko got ready to put the pieces back together.

"It'll be like another honeymoon," Tomoko said, giggling a little. They were both scared. In their absence their love for each other seemed to have grown, to become almost too huge for them to handle; it wasn't a simple animal passion anymore.

They were just about to make love when Matt heard a familiar voice at the door. "Matt, can I come in? I don't want to sleep alone anymore."

"Who is it, honey?" Tomoko said, pulling Matt into a hard, passionate embrace.

The voice in the doorway: "I had another dream. I dreamed that you sent me away."

"Can't he come back later?" Tomoko whispered.

"I think . . . he's worried about you and me. He needs someone to tell him he's still wanted. He's pretty insecure . . . can you blame him? He saw the Visitors eating his own mother!"

"Don't remind me," Tomoko said.

Matt thought of Tomoko as the main course in some Visitor banquet. It was not a comforting thought. He said, "CB, you can stay."

"That, Matthew Jones," said his wife, "is the first time I have ever known you to refuse sex! You have certainly changed."

"Welcome to motherhood!" Matt said laughing. And kissed Tomoko lightly on the cheek. CB came into the room, and the three clung tightly to each other, drawing from one another the only solace that was left to them.

Matt fell asleep to the sound of his adopted child's troubled breathing and to the whimpering of his wife, trapped in some nightmare of remembrance.

Chapter 9

"Leave me now."

Ogawa turned to dismiss his retinue. It was a nuisance to have to go about the city with an armed escort, but now that they had descended into a deserted section of Tokyo's labyrinthine subway system, it was no longer necessary to make an impression on anyone.

The right impression was so important.

The four guardsmen touched the hilts of their *katanas*, bowed, and left the minister of culture alone.

Presently a subway train came rolling into the station. It was, as Ogawa knew it would be, empty. The subway ran rarely in Tokyo now; only the Ueno Line and the Yamanote Line were still operational, and these only sporadically. And this station was nowhere near those two lines.

No.

Only the masters knew about this station.

And the train that pulled up . . . it did not bear the familiar ideographs that indicated a train's destination or what line it was running on. No. Instead, on a circle of crimson, there was inscribed a familiar symbol in an extraterrestrial language. A symbol that, if seen by any normal person, would have struck immediate terror in his heart.

Ogawa was not afraid.

He was not an ordinary person. Far from it.

Once upon a time, of course, he had been a mere human being: a minor government bureaucrat, concerned with his job and with pleasing his superiors and with saving enough money to buy trinkets for his mistress and videotapes for his wife. What a dreadful time that had been! Always something to worry about, some petty, insignificant problem.

He was happy now.

When he had problems to worry about now, they were big problems. Like reshaping Japan in the proper image. Like paving the way for the return of the masters . . . for bringing Earth into the hegemony of a galactic empire. Big, big things; visions and destinies worthy of his imagination, worthy of his ambition.

Of course, he'd had to pay a price for all this—days of agony in one of their conversion chambers. The thought nagged at him a little as he straightened his tie and fiddled with his mustache. He had to look perfect for this meeting. Oh, the agony! But it was a good price for becoming almost like one of the masters himself. As close to godlike as a human being could get.

The train waited patiently for him. Of course. He was its only passenger; it had been sent for him. How things had improved since the days of being a bureaucrat! Satisfied that his appearance would be neat enough to render his interview as unobtrusive as possible, he stepped into the nearest car, sat down, and waited.

Guards blindfolded him and took him down many corridors. He lost track of them. But the masters knew what was right. It was in his own interests that the masters would not let him see the way. Doubtless it would only serve to clutter up a mind that should be devoted only to a single thing: utter subservience. It was a wonderful thing, this complete obedience. It was the vow a samurai used to take to his feudal lord. It was, indeed, a profoundly Zen-like thing.

How happy I am, he told himself over and over, as they

marched him deeper and deeper into what he imagined was the masters' stronghold.

At last they took away his blindfold. He was in a traditional Japanese reception chamber. A woman, obviously converted, knelt down to take his shoes and bowed as he climbed up a few steps onto the tatami-covered floor.

In front of him was a large screen of intricately painted lacquer. The design was a traditional one from China: a depiction of dragons frolicking in the sunlight, above the sea. Two humans cowered in terror, their rickety boat buffeted by the waves.

He bowed before the screen, squatting uncomfortably on the tatami as green tea was served to him in a courteous and elegant manner.

A voice came from behind the screen: "Ogawa."

"Hai, tono!" he said, addressing the voice by a title traditionally reserved for feudal lords. "But—"

He heard hands clapping. The screen was quickly folded by black-robed attendants. Sitting on the dais, decked in a silken kimono on which was dexterously handpainted the insignia of the *Bijitaa* high command, was a woman.

"My lady, I was expecting—"

"Fieh Chan?" She frowned. Her face darkened. He hoped he had not said the wrong thing. In spite of his conversion, Ogawa still felt a twinge of reluctance at the possibility that he might be commanded to commit *seppuku* for the cause of the masters. "Fieh Chan is not available."

"But, my lady—"

"I am called Murasaki. I am Fieh Chan's second in command. Unthinkable, that you should feel yourself worthy of a personal interview with the leader himself!" She sipped daintily from a teabowl. "Fieh Chan sees no one now."

"But Lady Murasaki, I have not seen him for four months. Not since . . ."

"Rest assured!" said the Visitor woman. "All is well. Let me hear your report."

"I humbly beg the Lady Murasaki's pardon," Ogawa

said, bowing so that his head knocked against the floor, "but I was given to understand that the Lord Fieh Chan wished to hear my information . . . in strictest confidence."

"Ah . . ." said Lady Murasaki menacingly. Her voice betrayed just a hint of that almost electronic quality that the Visitors seemed to acquire when their emotions were stirred, as though at those moments not quite able to contain their godlike nature within the limits of the human soma. "But Fieh Chan is visiting the Hong Kong sector at the moment. You know that an overlord such as he is so important that he is in charge of more than one district."

"Of course, my lady," Ogawa said, cringing in abject humility.

"Perhaps," Murasaki said, "you might care for a bite to eat?" She clapped her hands. "The *sashimi* is . . . exceptionally fresh today."

A servant with a tray crawled in. Bowing, he set one in front of Lady Murasaki and one in front of Ogawa. A covered bowl, ceramic, in the traditional Oriental blue-and-white glaze. "You are too kind, *tono*," he murmured.

A ratchety, scratching sound came from inside the bowl, like someone shaking up the *i ching* sticks for a divination.

"Eat, eat," said his hostess angrily.

He peeked inside the bowl. A claw shot out: pincers, fibrillating antennae. Lady Murasaki cackled hideously as she pulled the squirming lobster from her own bowl and began methodically to eat it, her tongue flicking furiously about to quell its feeble attempts at escape. Ogawa listened to the crunching of the shell, a lump in his throat.

"Ah, but you do not eat?"

"My lady, I—" He continued to eye her lobster nervously.

"Perhaps you'd care for a mouse?" she said, pulling one out of another covered dish and suspending it by its tail inside her mouth. He heard a squeal or two, an obscene gurgling sound, and then a single, muscular crunch. "Your world is so rich in delicacies," Murasaki said. A sadistic smile played across her face for a moment. "Perhaps you would like to join them?"

He looked wildly around. Two men in samurai costume had suddenly appeared and were standing on either side of him with their swords upraised.

"Or perhaps you would prefer the pleasures of another sojourn in the conversion chamber?"

The lobster had crawled out of his bowl now and was inching its way across the tray, working its pincers. If he didn't move, the crustacean would soon be crawling up his bent knees.

"Charming, Ogawa-san. At your age, still playing with your food."

He tried to keep his face composed as he madly jerked his knee and tried to shoo the lobster away with his hands.

"Now, let us understand one another fully, Ogawa-san! You will no longer answer to Fieh Chan. He is too exalted to deal with the likes of you."

"Yes, of course, my lady," said Ogawa, prostrating himself fully as he managed to fling the lobster away from him in the direction of Murasaki's dais. It landed at her feet. She regarded it coolly.

"Such impudence," she whispered menacingly. Then she bent down a little way, shot out her tongue to its full hideous length, and rolled it around the lobster as it attempted to scuttle away. Ogawa could not watch her devour a second one; he kept his face to the ground.

"As I have said, you will report only to me. And now, as to the plans regarding the grand masters of martial arts from all over the planet . . ."

"All proceeds apace, *tono*," he said.

"And the manufacture of the molecular pressure skins, according to Fieh Chan's inimitable design?"

"I humbly beg to inform you, my lady, that there is a shortage of raw materials. Our factory is vastly understaffed owing to your overseers' "—he choked—"feeding habits. There is but a single prototype DNA-analogue mold against which all the cellular material has to be cloned. If you could provide a few more of the prototype units, they could be grown much faster. Could not Fieh Chan provide some? Or even the formula, so that our scientists could duplicate it?"

"Fool! You dare to question us?" But Ogawa detected, suddenly, a note of uncertainty in her voice. Had something gone wrong, terribly wrong, in the overlords' hierarchy? Was that why they were unable to obtain the correct reagents to create enough of the pressure skins Fieh Chan had invented, which could protect the Visitors from the red dust? Was there some other, unrevealed reason why Fieh Chan could not come out and talk to him as they had always done in the old days? Fieh Chan had never toyed with him in this callous manner. Though there was no question of which was master and which was slave, Fieh Chan had always used him with a certain measure of politeness, almost cordiality. Certainly he had not addressed him with the pronoun *omae*, which reduced him to the stature of a child or an animal, but with the form *kimi*, which, while not actually polite, at least accorded him the status of an equal, a friend almost. The brusque words *omae* and *ore* fell most ungracefully from the lips of one who had assumed a woman's form, and Ogawa had to remind himself that the masters took whatever forms they chose, and whether they were themselves male and female or something altogether different was a matter of some conjecture.

What had gone wrong with the masters? Why had they been unable to provide him with materials that indeed would work to their own advantage? He had heard rumors, vicious and unfounded of course, that there had been some sort of coup in the highest ranks of the Far Eastern high command. Could it be that the masters were actually arguing among themselves?

At the moment a warning signal went off in Ogawa's mind. His brain was burning, burning . . . the conversion! He was having dangerous thoughts, evil thoughts. How could he possibly question the masters, the most beneficent and wise of all creatures? The pain came, pounding at his skull, the terrible burning, like nails of fire being driven into his neck. Oh, it was terrible! How could he have had such disloyal thoughts? How shameful! He did not deserve to live.

"My lady," he whispered huskily, "I have just had a disloyal thought. The only honorable course I have is suicide. I ask your permission—"

"Denied!" said the Lady Murasaki.

That was the worst punishment of all, to compel him to go on living with his shame.

Chapter 10

Matt, Tomoko, CB, and Anne Williams. What an unlikely quartet of heroes, Matt thought, to save the world. It was just like one of CB's fantasies about Batman and Robin coming true.

The four of them were sitting in the office once more. It was clear that they had a huge problem on their hands; but what could they do about it? Tomoko suggested trying to contact ex-members of the resistance.

"CB's the only one of us who knows anyone who used to be in the resistance," Matt said. "And we know what happened to Sean."

"Don't remind me," CB said.

"I have something to confess," Tomoko said, "which may be irrelevant, but . . ."

"Shoot," said Matt.

"When I was alone with Fieh Chan, he inquired about you; and I told him about your martial arts connections—"

"That's it! It's Japan!" Anne said. "Fieh Chan is behind it, and they're kidnapping the grand masters and taking them to Japan."

"Sounds dumb to me," said CB.

"Is it any dumber than banning Godzilla, for Christ's sake?" said Anne.

"Well, what can *we* do about it if it's something on that scale? So we call the cops," Matt said, "and say, look, a bunch of lizard ninjas are abducting the great martial arts experts of America—"

"The world, maybe," Anne said. "Have you called any of our colleagues in Europe?"

"You know the phone system's not all the way back to normal yet," Matt said.

"Casilli, Yasutake, and maybe Nakashima—that's all we know of." Anne pulled out the martial arts directory from the desk and began to page through it.

Three hours later they had their figures. Out of twenty-five people they called, nineteen had received the mysterious telegrams; fully seven had already vanished. Some of them were people Matt knew of only by reputation. Others Matt had actually fought in tournaments and exhibitions.

As the hours dragged on, Matt suddenly realized that they hadn't had anything to eat all day.

"Hold it. I'm going to call over to Po Sam's and order carryout." He picked up the phone.

"Just like old times," Tomoko said.

"I'll go," Anne said.

"Be careful," Matt said before telling Sam to produce four orders of whatever he was making today.

"Careful?" Anne said. "What can happen? I'll be gone for five minutes." She pulled her headband tighter and retied it.

Twenty minutes later, Matt said, "What's the matter with her?"

After ten more minutes they all went to the front door. They saw the parking lot of the shopping plaza, almost carless at the moment. In the middle of the lot—

There was a circle of black-garbed figures. At its center, Anne was standing, tensed into a tigerlike position, her hands clawing the air, her eyes fiery. The assassins circled, circled, taunting, coming closer, trying to draw her into combat.

"Let's go for it, CB!" Matt shouted.

The door was locked or blocked or something, even though they hadn't locked it that morning. Someone must have sabotaged it. "Get the hatchet." CB sprinted down the corridor; there was a hatchet, under glass, by the fire alarm. As the sound of shattering glass echoed down the hallway, Matt saw—

The fighters had gathered in a V-formation, backing Anne up against the wall of Po Sam's Diner! Within the diner he could see Sam cowering in terror and Theresa, Sam's wife, pulling a butcher knife down from a rack.

The first attacker charged. Anne tucked herself into a ball of energy and then seemed to explode outward in a cloud of fists and feet, sending the man smashing against a parked car. But two more had taken advantage of her attack to sneak up behind her. She was too quick. She swerved, flew at the two of them, tripped one so that he fell over and tripped the other. Then she changed postures, tensed her hands up so that they resembled the heads of serpents, cocked her elbows. She looked like a two-headed snake, coiling, darting, teasing. The others circled.

"She's got them under control, looks like," CB said, handing Matt the hatchet.

Matt started to hack away at the door. "I've got to get to her!" he shouted. "It's me they're after, not her—"

The door wasn't giving away very easily . . . it had been built strong. Matt had paranoically insisted on the Institute being virtually impregnable when they had bought the building and redesigned it. . . .

The remaining assailants were advancing now. One sprang! Anne dodged, her hands darted out to block the path of another while with her feet she kicked down one of the prone attackers who had been endeavoring to stand up. Matt could see the slick sweat on her neck, the pulsing muscles of her arm. She was good at what she did, he thought. How long could she keep it up, though?

The door was finally cracking now. There had been some kind of bolt jamming it . . . it fell off now and skidded onto the pavement . . . Matt saw that it was some device he'd never seen before . . . of alien manufacture maybe. Silvery and circular. Some of that lizard super-technology! He didn't have time to reflect on it. He cried out, "We're coming, Anne! Just hold them off for another second—" and ran out.

Anne looked up. For a split second she was defenseless—

Then he heard it. A whirring, whining sound, like a distant flute. And saw it slice the air: a whirling thing of blades, dazzling in the afternoon sun . . . soaring in a perfect arc, utterly beautiful, utterly deadly. "No!" he shouted.

And ran unthinking straight towards her . . . as the throwing star ripped into Anne's neck . . . a splatter of blood on the window of Po Sam's Diner . . . It's my fault, he thought, if only I hadn't called to her, attracted her attention—

Then: I'm surrounded!

Unthinkingly he had walked into the thick of them. Each had drawn a weapon. He looked from one to the other . . . their eyes glinted oddly in the sunlight, betraying something unmistakably alien. . . .

"You're all lizards, you're goddamn lizards!" he cried. He felt the anger now, he wanted to explode, he thought of his years of discipline and wanted to forget them all in his fury, then he forced himself to concentrate all his burning hatred into one ball, one knot, deep, deep inside himself . . . a split second of icy stillness as he waited for the spirits of his masters to possess him . . . then . . . outward! Lines of power unreeling endlessly from within as his fists became doorways into a universe of limitless energy . . . an animal howl of rage burst from his lips as he attacked—

The aliens rushed him all at once . . . he saw the glint of metal, knew he was unarmed, and taunted them: "Ten aliens with daggers can't beat one human being with nothing!" And laid into the first one, knocking him flat and rending the sheath of plastic that he knew would cause them to be exposed to the red dust and die. He didn't listen as the

Visitor within the disguise began to char and sizzle and fibrillate and screech in its metallic, abrasive language—

"No weapons!" he heard one shouting in English. "We take him alive! Just stun him for shipping!"

He didn't have time to react. More and more of them seemed to have popped up from behind parked cars and around the corner of the plaza. The only way he could go was backward, one agonizing step at a time, in the direction where Anne lay, blood spurting from her wound. He stepped on something . . . the remains of a Visitor? He didn't want to look.

There were just too many of them.

"What do you want to do with me?" he shouted. "Why are you so interested in capturing me?"

They didn't speak. They just kept on advancing. . . .

He saw CB come forward out of the gash in the door of the Institute, a frail slender figure, his face frozen into a grimace of determined ferocity, his body tense. "Stay back, kid!" Matt shouted. "This isn't any of your business— you'll just get killed, is all!"

At once they turned, like robots. The kid was trembling. "I gotta help you," he screamed, his voice shrill.

One of the aliens lifted his arm. It contained another throwing star. No, not that! Matt thought. They're going to kill him! He propelled himself forward, trying to reach the attacker before the star flew from his fingers . . . too late!

For an eternity it seemed to spin in the air. Its light hurt his eyes. . . .

Then he heard a *clunk* . . . he squeezed his eyes tight shut for a second, he didn't want to see . . . then scattered cries, the swish of something thin and metallic slicing the air. . . .

A hideous dying howl from the one who had thrown the star. It had glanced off something hard and gone whizzing back on its path and had impaled the creature's forehead, riving the protective plastic sheath and causing him to fall writhing to the ground.

What had stopped the star?

He saw.

An old man with a sword was standing in the middle of the parking lot. He wore a samurai helmet and full battle armor of a kind that Matt had only seen in Japanese movies.

The attackers—there were over a dozen of them—looked from Matt to the stranger in wild confusion. The stranger held his sword high, its hilt erect and level with his head, for a moment that seemed to last forever.

Then, uttering a terrifying bellow, he ran forward and with a single whirl had decapitated two of the attackers.

"Right on!" Matt cried, as he used the diversion to cartwheel into the huddle of perplexed lizard-men and began to flail at them with his fists and feet.

The stranger stood as if frozen, watching the whole thing with an expression half sad, half amused. Then, without warning, the sword flew out again. It sliced cleanly, mercilessly. The lizard ninjas didn't even have time to scream. One, two, three, they fell, like dominoes, as the old man moved, seeming to take his time, with the elegance of a kabuki actor, utterly cool. Each fling of the sword seemed to take only a flick of the wrist, yet Matt knew from his training that this required the utmost concentrated strength and inner discipline.

At last they lay in heaps on the parking lot pavement . . . their flesh dissolving as the air touched them. Matt couldn't bear to watch. He just ran forward into the arms of his wife and the kid.

The old man was silent for a long time. Then he walked over to where Anne lay. Sam from the restaurant and his wife Theresa had come out; they were standing in the doorway of the diner, wringing their hands helplessly.

The old man knelt down by Anne. Gently he touched her; listened to her heart, as Matt, CB and Tomoko gathered around. At last he said, "I am sorry."

"She's . . ." Tomoko said.

"Yes. I am sorry."

"Shit, I'm going to kill them," CB whispered fiercely.

"Do not be angry, young man," the old man said to the

kid. His eyes were full of kindness. How strange, Matt thought, that he should seem to exude such compassion . . . when he's shown himself to be such a master of violence. The old man took his helmet off. His forehead was drenched with sweat, his sparse hair matted. "Anger is not good," he continued. "Inner peace; that is what you must have. You must feel a kind of pity—love, even—for your foe. It is not his fault that his karma has pitted him against you."

"What are you, one of those hare krishna types?" Matt said belligerently. For he had always taught himself to discipline his anger, to turn it into raw force . . . never to eliminate it.

"Hardly," said the swordsman.

"You're from Japan?" CB said. Matt could see the stars of hero-worship in the boy's eyes, and he felt strangely jealous.

"Yes. My name is Kenzo Sugihara," he said. "I am a swordsman."

"I can see that!" Matt said. "You're one of the best I've ever seen. I wish I'd known about you before. I wonder why I've never heard of you?" Matt was a little suspicious. Or maybe it was his jealousy speaking. "I've either met or at least heard of every grand master of every major martial arts style in the world. . . ."

Sugihara laughed. "Who says I am a grand master?" he said. "My art is only in my heart, not in some shelf full of trophies or some certificate from an institution."

Again, Matt felt strangely stung by this, although he knew there was no real justification. The old man made him so uneasy. He couldn't put his finger on what it was that was gnawing away at the back of his mind. "Why are you here?" he said.

"I have come to help you," Sugihara said. "I have no reason to love the Visitors. I have every reason to believe that you and I can help each other. Once I was their captive; I have learned much of their ways."

"You know what they're up to? You know where they're

taking the grand masters?" Tomoko said. "I overheard one of them saying about Matt, not to kill him, only to 'stun him for shipping.' That sounded ominous."

"I don't know the whole story. Only that they are taking them to Japan. So to stop them, we would have to go there ourselves."

"Can't we call the U.S. army or something? Isn't the Pentagon going to do something?" Matt said.

"I . . . have some small influence in these matters. I telephoned some . . . important people. They told me that the United States is not at war with Japan, and that in any case, human beings are in the government there, not Visitors. They do not want to face the fact that some Visitors may have found a way of returning, of shielding themselves from the red dust."

"But it's out of our hands," said Matt. "All we can do is . . . hole up somewhere until it blows over. Right?"

"You will soon stand at a karmic crossroads in your life. In one direction is the way to riches, a moderate, well-deserved reputation, a loving wife . . . a comfortable retirement. But in this scenario there will be one cloud: at any moment, without warning, aliens will swoop down and devour you or enslave you. It probably won't ever happen . . . you will probably always be happy."

"And the other path?" Matt said. But he already knew. He just didn't want to have to say it himself; it was too vast to contemplate right now.

"The other path . . ." The old man shook his head ruefully. "You will go to Japan. You and I and perhaps your wife, who speaks Japanese, and this child—for if he stays he will surely be in grave danger. The perils you will face will be immense. But the reward will be freedom, Matthew Jones; freedom from the alien threat, for all your people."

"I don't know what you're talking about," Matt said slowly, still reluctant to face all that had happened.

"Anne's dead," CB said. "She was our friend. I wanna go over there and kick ass!" He wasn't frightened anymore,

Matt saw. His face was distorted with grief and rage; these new emotions had dispelled all his terror.

Tomoko said, "But I just escaped from there . . . do I really have to go back? Is Fieh Chan still in power?"

The old man looked into her eyes. "That I cannot answer," he said. There was a long pause, each of them cocooned in his private thoughts.

"Thank you for saving my husband's life," Tomoko said finally. Matt felt a sudden pang of guilt at having forgotten this simplest of courtesies when he might well be dead or worse by now. . . .

The old man and Tomoko continued to look into each other's eyes. Are my feelings tricking me? Matt thought. I could swear that they *know* each other . . . that there's something between them! My family, my family, he thought . . . the three of us have been together for less than twenty-four hours, and already I'm going to lose them to this bizarre old man who has come from God knows where. . . .

Later he wouldn't know whether it was jealousy or courage that motivated him. He wouldn't remember whether it was his desire to save the human race from whatever it was that menaced it, or some selfish yearning to be a greater hero than this old man, to really show his wife and kid what kind of stuff he was made of. It was all these things, and more: his love for his friend, lying there in a pool of her own blood; his concern for the grand masters, captured and taken who knows where; the fact that his life was going nowhere, that he was stuck in a rut. Being a hero, he was to realize later, wasn't simple, wasn't like in comic books or TV shows. It was damn complicated.

At the time he just stood for a while, while the others looked expectantly at him, waiting for him to say something. At the back of his mind, a childish little voice was going eeny-meeny-mino-mo, she loves me, she loves me not. . . .

"Yes," he said. For a moment he wasn't sure whether he'd just said yes or no.

Chapter 11

A room in a secret location: a small room, bare and sparsely furnished: a tatami floor, a sleeping area separated by screens, a low table with a few ornaments, a *shoji* screen that opened out to reveal a traditional stone garden . . . and on the other side of the room, a wall-sized video monitor.

In front of it sat the Visitor known as Lady Murasaki, fiddling with some controls that seemed to produce nothing but static. Murasaki seemed to become more and more frustrated.

On the table next to the control console and the ornaments . . . a small plate of human fingers, half nibbled, and a steaming bowl of hot green tea.

At last an image formed on the screen.

"Ah, Wu Piao," she purred. "I have been trying to contact you for days."

"Murasaki!" said the man in the other screen. He wore a Mao shirt, fastidiously buttoned to the top, and a beret, both of them bearing the insignia of the Visitors. "What a pleasant surprise." From his tone, it was clear that her communication was neither a surprise nor pleasant. "I have been attempting to make contact, but . . . as you well know, technology hasn't been quite the same around this mud-eating planet since the main fleet was forced to depart. I've had to jury-rig this device with spare parts rifled from—a television broadcasting station, they call it—here in Hong Kong."

"I demand to speak to Fieh Chan!" Murasaki said.

"That won't be possible," Wu Piao said.

"I accuse you of hiding him from us." The interview with that weak, contemptible earthling Ogawa had upset Murasaki more than she cared to admit to herself. For one thing, he had come dangerously close to guessing the truth. It was lucky that his conditioning had kicked on just in time . . . or she would have been forced to kill him. That would have been inconvenient, with things in the mess they were.

"We are not hiding him," said Wu Piao. "We keep getting messages that purport to be from him, but we can't locate him. Meanwhile, production of the pressure skin-thermal generators has come to a standstill."

"Sometimes I envy these miserable apes," Murasaki said. "They lack our deviousness. Of course Fieh Chan did not disclose the details of his invention to anyone! He wanted to use it as new clout—to block *my* accession to power in our hierarchy! Now he's staged this bizarre disappearance in order to convince the high command that he's indispensable. He's just waiting for us to bungle so that he can inveigle himself further up the ladder."

"Have you tried analyzing them?" Wu Piao said coldly.

"We are very short of science staff, as you well know." Murasaki saw that her colleague was searching for a chink in her defenses. She could not afford to let him see any weakness. Angrily she plucked a finger from the dish and began chomping on it. The food was the one good thing about this world, she reflected. With its extravagant, luxurious vegetation, its copious water, its profusion of life forms, all blossoming and reproducing with reckless abandon, this planet's lack of restraint was profoundly disturbing to her sensibilities. She thought of the deserts of her home world, the harsh extremes, the constant drought. Ah, but the home world had a severe purity that all this craziness could never match.

"You do not speak?" asked Wu Piao.

"I was thinking of Fieh Chan. I never could understand his motivations." She chose her words carefully; it was her intention to poison Wu Piao's mind, but also to exonerate herself from any accusation of having done so if Fieh Chan should happen to return. Her own suspicion—and hope— was that he had somehow really succumbed to the red dust, that the experimental pressure skin he had himself designed had somehow malfunctioned. How she hated him for foreseeing the possibility that the humans would use bacteriological warfare! She had advised him time and time again that the Earth creatures were far too stupid to think of such a thing . . . and yet they had somehow done it anyway. That apes should by some fluke give the appearance of acting with the intelligence of reptiles rankled her. That Fieh Chan should have made such a wild prediction, and gone ahead and designed a countermeasure without letting anyone else know the secret of it, and *then* be proven right! And he had actually fraternized with the humans, actually gone so far as to study this Zen philosophy, as they called it, a philosophy dangerously close to the banned *preta-na-ma* religion. Horrible, horrible! What a despicable person! And that she should have been passed over for the command of the Far Eastern sector in favor of that ape-loving heretic! She thought of how best to present her insinuations to her colleague Wu Piao. Together they might be able to manipulate the high command into making her leadership position official—if Fieh Chan didn't come wandering back.

Then there was the possibility that Wu Piao knew exactly where Fieh Chan was, that they were involved in a plot against her. Perhaps they were manufacturing the thermal pressure skins in a factory in Hong Kong right now, and Wu Piao was laughing at her behind her back. Was he really so subtle?

"Tell me," she said sweetly, daintily sucking the last shred of marrow from the finger's bones and tossing it idly back onto the plate, "did Fieh Chan ever mention *preta-na-ma* to you?"

An expression of consummate horror crossed Wu Piao's face. *How well he acts!* thought Murasaki, who knew, from breaking into his computer dossier, that he had once, as a young saurian, attended a secret meeting of the underground cult of peace and intraspecies brotherhood.

"I don't think so," he said cautiously.

But with that single question, she knew that she had sent his mind racing. For *preta-na-ma* was one of the most taboo words in their language; as a result, it was one of the most powerful. He was on the defensive now; undoubtedly he knew she knew about possible subversive behavior in his youth. She said, "Find Fieh Chan. Get his secret from him. Time is short. Technology is primitive here, even more primitive since we destroyed their economies and many of their arsenals. We can't recharge our lasers or reach the Mother Ships for fresh supplies. I am developing alternative methods. But we need more pressure skins." These were obvious truths; she did not mind admitting them to Wu Piao. She would lose no ground here.

"Isn't it possible that the formula you are seeking is concealed in your own computer?"

"It may well be. But if so, it is keyed to some code that we have been unable to uncover," she said. She quickly added, "We are close to it." Though nothing of the sort was true, and they both knew it.

"And your alternative weaponry? What sort of thing is that?" Wu Piao said. The mocking tone in his voice was unmistakable. *He thinks he has me on the run!* she thought. *Why, what impertinence!*

"It is something we are stealing from the apes themselves," she said at last. "Something primitive, but then we should not, despite our sophistication, necessarily reject the primitive within ourselves. We should not forget the myth of the temptress ape! And just because apes invented it," she added self-righteously, "doesn't mean we can't improve on it. They don't have our technological advantages; they're not as intelligent as us. So think of what we can do with one of their inventions."

"Sounds nebulous to me. You are floundering, Murasaki, grasping at straws. What are you trying to learn from these humans—mystical rites? Voodoo? And," he added, "it was you who first brought up *preta-na-ma*, not I. Perhaps you'd care to confess to being a practitioner? You know what the punishment is."

"Be silent! I am still above you in the chain of command—until other orders come. I demand respect. I will not brook so heinous an accusation."

"The chain is broken, my dear Lady Murasaki. The Mother Ships cannot reach us at present. The future depends on our individual initiative, not on paying lip service to the high command! When the ships return, they'll look at results before the promotions are dealt out."

"When they return," Murasaki said. "Yes, when they return." It was a ritual; it signified that the conversation was over.

"Yes. When the Mother Ships return," said Wu Piao, sighing, and vanished in a cloud of video static.

Chapter 12

The sun was setting over Haataja Plaza, behind the freeway overpass that arced up off of Spruce. They were sitting in Po Sam's. "We might as well get bombed out of our minds," Matt was saying, downing another bottle of Tsing Tao beer. "I thought everything would return to normal after the Visitors left."

"But nothing's normal!" Theresa, Sam's wife, moaned. "Police not coming to investigate Anne's death, no coroner, no nothing—nobody interested!"

"How are we even going to get to Japan?" Tomoko said. "If the evidence really does point to some plot that has its origins there. You know I had to wait months for clearance to leave Tokyo. I'll bet CB doesn't even have a passport. Matt, have you been out of the country since the invasion? I'll bet no one has."

"I guess I never thought about that," Matt said, beginning to regret his hasty yes and hoping against hope there would be a way out. "What are we supposed to do, call up TWA at LAX and book a flight? I don't even have enough left on my credit cards for all four of us."

"How can you think of credit cards at a time like this?" Tomoko said.

"We will not leave from LAX," said Sugihara suddenly, using the common nickname for Los Angeles' largest international airport. Everyone looked up to where he was

82

standing; his voice, though exceptionally quiet, radiated that kind of authority. "There is only one official plane a week to Tokyo. The Japanese government has decided to close its borders, for mysterious reasons all its own. Only a few are allowed to take the weekly transport. There are no scheduled commercial flights like in the days before the invasion."

He stepped away from the video game machine. Apparently CB had been showing him the trick with the game. He was impressive in the dingy diner. The dim light striped his face with shadow and the metal fiber in his samurai costume glowed. How on earth, Matt wondered, had a man dressed like this managed to materialize in a shopping plaza in suburbia without exciting any comment? Downtown, on the Boulevard, now, that was another matter, but Haataja and L.A. were like different universes.

"There are things I know about the Visitors that I was able to glean during my captivity," Sugihara said. "I know, for example, that one of the Visitors' most brilliant scientists—Fieh Chan himself, it is rumored—designed a thermal molecular pressure skin, a semi-organic, extremely thin and pliable body sheath that can be worn by Visitors, is invisible, and is impermeable to the red dust. I have heard, also, that for some reason I cannot exactly establish, the supply of these pressure skins is short. They are malleable and flexible enough when not mistreated, but can be punctured fairly easily. This is fatal."

"That explains what I found on the one I killed last night," Matt said.

"I also know that a number of saurian agents have come to America; that they have a base right here in Orange County at John Wayne Airport."

"That airport's been closed ever since . . . the invasion!" Tomoko said. "It's still closed."

"Precisely," Sugihara said.

There was such serenity in his face. Matt couldn't understand it, didn't like it. And what was this between the old man and his wife? Had they met before in Japan? And how had he so bewitched the kid? It had taken Matt months to win him over. Resentment flooded his mind. "How the hell do you know so much about these damn aliens?" Matt demanded. "Tell me, if you know so much, who's this alien swordmaster they keep sending me telegrams about?"

"I could not tell you," Sugihara said. "It is a mystery."

"How do I know you're not a collaborator, or even worse?"

Tomoko said, "For God's sake! The man just saved your life, Matt."

"I don't like any of it."

"You have given your word, Matt Jones, that you will join in an expedition to find the cause of these disappearances, possibly to rescue your friends and colleagues."

"Is that what I've done?" Matt said. "I agreed to no such thing! I was confused. I . . ." He stopped, flustered.

"I give you my word as a swordmaster that I am not your enemy, Matt Jones."

"What if you *are* working for the—the *things*? Then your word won't be worth a nickel!"

"That is a risk you will have to take. Just as I take it of you, who have given your word to come with me."

"I suppose . . ."

"We'll go," Tomoko said.

"What about Anne's funeral?" Matt said with a twinge of desperation.

"We take care funeral," said Sam. "You have much pain in your heart, Matt. It is good you go. You must wash away pain. Believe old Sam. I think Anne want you go. Because she die fighting them."

"I have a plan," Sugihara said. "I cannot implement it alone. Tomorrow we will go down to the John Wayne Airport. A Visitor craft, one of the few yet remaining on this planet, is there. They have been using it to transport certain—"

"You mean Rod Casilli? and Kunio Yasutake? and Lex

Nakashima? and Jonathan Kippax and all the other grand masters?" Matt said.

"I fear so."

"Go on."

"I have been able to ascertain that this Visitor craft will be departing Orange County tomorrow, en route to Tokyo. The Visitors have been gathering certain—what they euphemistically refer to as 'raw materials.' We can be on that craft. I believe that I can bluff my way on board. I am familiar enough with their ways so that I can pretend to be one of them."

"And us?"

"You will have to be my prisoners, I'm afraid."

"It's a trick!" Matt said. "You *are* working for them. You've got to be!"

Sugihara stood very erect; his face betrayed no emotion at all.

"What have we got to lose?" Tomoko said.

"That's a fine thing to say!" shouted Matt. "We've a lot to lose! Our business. Our shirts. Our lives. Each other."

"You do not trust me?" said Sugihara.

"No! I mean why the hell should I? You barge into my life, you steal the affections of my wife and kid—"

"So insecure, my friend?" said Sugihara. "I am so sorry. It is as your friend Sam has said: you carry too much pain in your heart. The way of Zen is not for all men, yet—Matt, please believe that I am not your enemy. Neither do I covet what is yours. The world—this entire planet, the lives of billions—the world is at stake!"

"The world," Matt repeated tonelessly. He knew he was just arguing for the sake of arguing; somehow or another they were all going, they were all going on this wild adventure.

He had given his word, hadn't he?

They didn't bother to go home that night; they just sacked out on exercise mats in the large and echoey main gymnasium of the Institute. They'd all made noises about going home and preparing for the journey; in the end they had been afraid to leave the building at night, afraid to encounter more of the ninja-garbed assailants.

Matt couldn't sleep. He got up, started to pace the corridor outside the hall, where Sugihara sat, his eyes closed, in a meditative position. Matt couldn't tell if he was asleep or awake. In the half dark there was a strange luminous pallor to his skin, almost as though it had been laminated, dipped in plastic. Could he be one of them? Why was he helping Matt and the others if not to lead them into an insidious trap?

He thought he heard a toilet flush; crept along the wall to take a look; saw Tomoko. "Can't sleep either?" she said.

"I don't trust him!" he whispered.

"I understand. But, I don't know why, I just do."

"Did you know him before? In Tokyo, I mean. How was he able to track us down like this? How did he manage to find us just in the nick of time? You *do* know him, don't you? I saw the way you two looked at each other." His jealousy came through again, he couldn't help it.

"I swear I've never seen him in my life," Tomoko said with such forcefulness that Matt knew she could not be lying to him. Tomoko had never been good at lying. Often, before their separation, it had been her inability to tell him comfortable lies that had infuriated him so much. And she had always had good instincts about people. He remembered that it was on her say-so that he'd hired Anne, who had turned out to be much more trustworthy than anyone he'd hired on his own.

"Oh, Matt, I do love you," she said softly.

"Yes. I do need to hear that." Only when he said it did Matt realize it for the first time. "I'm going off God knows where to fight God knows what. Oh, Tomoko . . ."

They kissed. So much remembered passion was in that kiss. . . .

"Let's make love," he urged.

"Now? Here?" She laughed, a gentle, loving laugh.

Suddenly—

He pricked up his ears. "Someone's in the office, talking."

"Shh. Yes. Let's investigate."

"No, you stay, I'll go."

"Together, Matt. From now on, always together." *She's changed too,* Matt thought. *It's not just me. We're both trying so much harder.*

They tiptoed into the outer office. The door of the inner office was ajar. There was a light on inside.

A little boy's voice: "No . . . I can't tell you where I'm going, Mia. It's like a secret, you know?"

"Who's Mia?" Tomoko whispered.

"His girlfriend," Matt said, grinning.

"At his age?"

"Kids."

"Listen."

". . . I mean like it's really big stuff and the phone might be bugged. If I don't see you for a while, it's casual, you know? Like I still like you. Hey. Oh, I found out something about 'Galaga?' Player one like turns over at a million minus one points, but there's extra spaces in front of the scoring line for player two, so like if you play doubles you can get totally boned on player one and then you won't turn over until a *billion* minus one so you can really jam, you know? Like totally rad."

"What the hell is he talking about?" Tomoko asked in amazement.

"Beats me," Matt said.

CB paused; he must have heard them whispering outside.

"Hey, later. Like my 'rents want me to go now."

"His 'rents?" Tomoko said. "He's playing landlord?"

"Shh," Matt said. "I think this is CB's equivalent of a mushy farewell scene."

"Oh."

They tiptoed away.

* * *

The van—which bore the logo of Matt's Institute—pulled up to a barricade at the airport. It was not quite dawn. Sugihara was driving. It turned out that he had a car parked in the lot of the Institute: a Ferrari, no less. That was how he had appeared so quickly. What a mess of contradictions the man was. In the morning he had pulled a little overnight bag out of his back seat, gone into the bathroom at the Institute, and reemerged wearing a Visitor uniform! Tomoko had screamed.

"Relax," he had said mildly. "I stole it." Then he had gone on to explain his plan. . . .

Matt, Tomoko, and the kid had had to submit to being tied up. Then packed into the van. And then, with considerable misgivings, Matt had turned over the keys of the van to Sugihara.

"*Arigato gozaimashita,*" the old man had said, bowing stiffly. "Now—you must act defiant, and perhaps a little frightened."

And they had driven off.

A man (man?) in the parking lot booth gave them only a cursory glance before admitting them. "You seem to know the way a little too well," Matt said suspiciously.

He looked out of the window and saw a bronze statue of John Wayne. He remembered the day they'd put up that statue and renamed the Orange County airport after a genuine American hero. *My* hero, Matt thought, remembering images out of his childhood. What would the Duke have done in my position? The light of the encroaching dawn caressed the statue; it shone, red-gold, like a beacon of hope.

"Who's that fat guy?" said CB.

"Damn kids! Don't know *anything* anymore. That, my boy, is a real hero—a real man!"

CB shrugged, and Matt wondered if he was getting too old.

They drove past an open gate—unattended—onto a

runway. Matt saw it then: a sleek, streamlined craft—a skyfighter, they called it on the newscasts.

Two or three guards were walking back and forth, patrolling.

Sugihara stopped the car.

"I have the prisoners," he said.

"Shi-i-it," CB whispered.

Matt's heart started pounding.

"All right." Sugihara said in a raspy whisper, "start acting the way I told you."

"I'm not acting!" Matt said. "You really tricked us, didn't you? I know your kind wouldn't be above expending a few lizards as a ruse to capture me."

"Silence!" Sugihara got out of the car. "Put these humans on board the skyfighter!" he commanded the guards.

"Trickster!" Matt hissed.

The guards stared at them. "We received no orders about prisoners," one began. "The other shipments have been ready for some time. Wait a minute, you're not the usual copilot!"

Sugihara transfixed him with a penetrating, hypnotic stare. The guard seemed to cringe. "Yes, master," he said abjectly. What was all that about? Then those outside walked out of earshot and Matt could hear, vaguely, that they were conversing rapidly and angrily. That was odd. Matt stored the memory in his mind, adding it to his suspicions.

The van door slid open. Matt was pulled roughly out and pushed up a little ramp into the skyfighter. They went down for Tomoko and CB, who struggled and made a lot of noise as they were shoved down beside Matt.

Matt looked around. The cargo was bizarre. There were cages full of rhesus monkeys, who whimpered and gazed sadly from side to side. There were bundles of books, some in the angular, incomprehensible alien script. There were cartons labeled with the polysyllabic names of organic chemicals, with the logo of a prominent pharmaceutical factory on them. There were rolls of what looked like clear acetate sheets.

Matt heard a brief whirring sound; then they took off.

After a while Tomoko said, "I'm sorry, Matt. I was wrong, I guess."

They were silent for a long time.

The skyfighter moved very smoothly. Even though he was uncomfortably tied up, Matt could hardly tell they were in motion. He could hear voices, but could not tell if they were human or if they had that harsh Visitor quality.

At last Sugihara came aft.

"Well, thank you for getting us killed," Matt said.

Without a word, Sugihara started to untie them. "Whoa!" Matt began.

Tomoko gave him an I-told-you-so look. CB grinned like an idiot. Sugihara put a finger to his lips.

Matt made a sign to the other two to wait there, then he and Sugihara crept forward. The two captors were relaxing at the control console. Matt and Sugihara rushed forward and simultaneously dealt them two karate chops. A single thud resounded in the small cabin. The two slumped forward. Sugihara's victim began to wheeze and emit the now familiar but still sickening sound as the toxin entered his body. However, the one Matt had struck just lay motionless. His face stayed exactly the same.

"He was a human being," Sugihara said.

"A human!—"

"A collaborator."

Anger—

"He could not help himself, Matt. Be compassionate. He was converted. He never had a choice after they entered his mind and stole his very soul from him." He had already begun methodically to undress the Visitor, heedless of the sticky rheum that dripped from what had been his body. "Quick, Matt. You must take the clothes off yours."

The prone human stirred.

"Hit him again!"

"I've never killed a human being," Matt said.

"This is a war," Sugihara said. He reached over and deftly snapped the man's neck with a single blow. "Now take his uniform."

Matt obeyed sullenly.

"There are bins aft that may contain laser rifles," Sugihara said. "Maybe some of them are charged up, although they've been able to do less and less of that lately. Quick, we'll have to toss the bodies."

"Where?" Matt asked.

"In the Pacific," Sugihara said, pointing at the view-screens that surrounded them. Matt saw the ocean—serene, cloud-kissed, beautiful. "By the way, does anyone know how to fly one of these things?"

"I do." Tomoko had come out of the back. She now moved to the console and sat calmly down as if she'd been doing it all her life.

"Where'd you learn to—" Matt began.

"Now this," said Tomoko, "is the altimeter. *That's* the fuel gauge."

"You're joking." Matt stared open-mouthed.

"No, darling. This is just a little something I picked up while I was trying to avoid being raped, killed and eaten."

"God, I feel like a useless appendage," Matt said. "I mean, here I am, twenty thousand feet above sea level. A samurai who looks like he's stepped out of a Kurosawa movie has concocted this outlandish plan, my wife has somehow learned to fly alien spacecraft, my kid—"

"Can cream you at 'Galaga' blindfolded," CB finished for him as he came out of the hold. "Hey, Sugihara-san, what's all that junk in the back *for?*"

"I would guess that the rhesus monkeys, being similar to humans, might have something to do with experiments? And the chemicals and things: something to do with the production of the pressure skins."

"I still think you know too much. I still think you're

pretty damn suspicious," Matt said, although he was
starting to like the fellow a lot more now that the plan was
becoming more clear. "So now I guess we land at Tokyo
airport and go in and report to the Japanese underground,
and then start kicking ass? That's who you're working for,
isn't it? The Japanese underground. Stands to reason."

"I cannot say," Sugihara said enigmatically.

On the whole, Matt was coming to the conclusion that
Sugihara's eccentricities were just that, eccentricities. Obviously the man had a very rich and full fantasy life and
enjoyed role-playing. Well, if he wanted to act out a role in
a costume epic, let him. As long as he got results.

They spent some time lugging the human corpse and the
limp saurian remains aft and flushing them into the air;
packing the uniforms away in backpacks that they found in
the equipment bins; testing the laser guns and rifles in order
to find some that still worked.

"How long till we land?" Matt repeated his question at
last, nervously eyeing Tomoko as she worked the controls
of the skyfighter. Would the Duke have allowed himself to
be bested by kids and women like this?

"Well," Sugihara said, "I've bad news. We don't
actually land."

"I knew it! You *are* one of them—" Matt started to panic
again.

"No, no, no. It's just that Narita Airport is crawling with
red tape, with Visitors, and with converted people. No, I'm
afraid we're going to have to arrive in a somewhat more
dramatic manner. Tomoko, where do they keep the parachutes in these things?"

"Parachute? Rad!" CB exclaimed.

"Parachute?" Matt said.

"Oh, don't worry, Matt darling," Tomoko said. "It's no
big deal, jumping out of alien skyfighters. I do it all the
time. Piece of cake."

Matt rolled his eyes.

PART THREE

TOKYO: THE CHASE

Chapter 13

Lying once more prostrate upon the tatami-covered floor, Minister Ogawa saw only the edge of an elaborately brocaded kimono. Upon a field of deep purple silk were stitched, in gold thread and filled in in garish reds and turquoises, scenes of unmitigated horror: lizards gnawing at the entrails of humans, lizards whose eyes were fiery yellow topazes sewn into the very lining of the robe. Beneath the outer kimono was a second and a third, each one more frightening than the last. It was a horrifying parody of the traditional Japanese bridal garments.

Ogawa kept his face firmly on the floor, breathing in the heavy scent of old wood and fresh straw.

"You do not look at my face?" the Lady Murasaki said.

"Master, your—your brilliance blinds me, I—"

"Look at me!"

He jerked up his head.

A scream escaped his lips, was quickly stifled, and he fell into the prostrate position once again.

In that split second he had seen—

She no longer even bothered to wear a human mask! Perched upon those impressive robes, the layer upon layer of brocade and fine fabrics, was the head of a reptile! And even as he retreated in horror he saw that Lady Murasaki had been daintily nibbling on—a human finger!

"You do not like my appearance?" said Lady Murasaki.

"I—you—my masters—"

"Orders have come from Fieh Chan. No more will we conceal our true natures from you lower beings. We are the lords and you the miserable serfs. No more of this masquerading. We need not lull your people into servile obedience, eh? We have *you* and other creatures like you to do the job for us. No. From now on we will concern ourselves only with the exercise of power: pure, naked, ineluctable power. Say it! Say that I am beautiful, that mine is the ideal form—that you are nothing but a lowly ape whose privilege it is to lift your filthy face from the dust and gaze with rapture into the face of a reptile—a truly sapient being—a god!"

Memories of the old days flashed through Ogawa's mind. He remembered his meetings with Fieh Chan. Fieh Chan had never made him feel so . . . so despicable. Never! At the back of his mind a tiny thought stirred and would not rest, though his conditioning reared up to combat it, to push it back into the furthest recesses of his unconscious so that he would never be aware that some part of him still longed for freedom. . . .

Quickly he began to murmur the words Murasaki had put into his mouth. "Yes, Lady Murasaki, your form is perfect, ineffable, and sublime. I am only an ape, I exist only to serve and feed you."

"Good. That's more like it. And now the conversion of the Matsuzakaya department store in the Ginza—it is complete? And the official announcements, they have been made?"

"Yes, my lady. Bills have been posted all over Tokyo about the new . . . self-destruction center. Please, my lady, give me the honor of being the first to use the facilities."

"Denied!" Lady Murasaki grated.

"But my shame—"

"You will entertain no more selfish thoughts of doing away with your own life, you pathetic little cur, until *I* so decide. I am your feudal lord. None other shall possess your life."

"*Hai, tono!*"

And Ogawa bowed and bowed, over and over, to the saurian creature who wore the robes of a lady of ancient lineage. . . .

Alone in the private chamber of the secret Visitor stronghold, Lady Murasaki could not resist calling Wu Piao to gloat.

"What!" Wu Piao said, taken aback. "You do not even bother with the human masks?" He still wore his, she saw in the static-filled screen.

"I am not an ape-lover like Fieh Chan," she said, wantonly disregarding the old policy of speaking a human language even when not in the humans' presence. "I'm not sexually attracted to them; I've no desire to look like one. Now that Fieh Chan has conveniently disappeared I see no reason to keep up the pretenses. I was never keen on the idea of toadying to these aliens in any way. Furthermore, now that we have to wear the thermal pressure skins to avoid exposure to the planet's contamination, it's just too inconvenient to wear the ape masks as well."

"You're taking a gamble," Wu Piao said in Japanese. *His caution,* Murasaki thought, *is touching to behold.*

"More than a gamble! Japan is entirely in my hands. Economy and technology have collapsed so much that it is entirely at my mercy. Its government is controlled by converts. I have already completed construction of a food-processing plant—taking advantage of these people's propensity for suicide! It's wonderful! We slaughter them and decontaminate them right there on the premises; then we process them."

"But we have no way of shipping the food home as yet!"

"Bah! When the home-world scientists discover a cure for this toxin—and I am sure they will soon, considering how much more advanced we are than they—*my* sector will be the springboard from which they will control this world—not Los Angeles. And *I* will at last have a shot at the high command itself! Not to mention making a tidy profit from the prepackaged food."

"Your ambition is admirable," said her colleague, and Murasaki noted with satisfaction the envy in Wu Piao's voice. "But what if Fieh Chan should return?"

"The possibility is negligible!" Murasaki responded haughtily. Wu Piao opened his mouth to object; she went on, "and I should not have to remind you that regulations state that in his absence, for whatever cause, his second officer has full authority to act in his behalf. And in this interim I happen to outrank you!"

"I didn't think," Wu Piao said as he faded from the screen, "that you'd let me forget that for long."

Chapter 14

Déjà vu. That was the prevailing feeling in Tomoko's mind. The falling out of the sky . . . the distant flash of the exploding skyfighter . . . the rice fields. Only, this time the sky wasn't red with toxin. The toxin had settled, seeped into the earth's foliage, penetrated its soil. And the rice was no longer the dayglo green of new rice, but a deeper color, dark green turning to yellow. In the distant hills, peasants toiled in the terraced rice farms.

CB and Matt kept looking around. The boy especially seemed moved to wonderment by the slightest thing.

Things had changed since the last time Tomoko had crash-landed outside Tokyo. There had been a few cars on the highway then; now there were none. They walked. There was an abandoned gas station, its phone out of commission. A sign read:

CLOSED
BY EDICT OF THE SUPREME DIET OF JAPAN
BY REASON OF THE GASOLINE CRISIS

"So they've been cut off from the rest of the world," Matt said when Sugihara had finished translating the hasty calligraphy of the billboard.

"Let's hurry on," Tomoko said. "If we're lucky we may reach the subway system by nightfall."

"What'll we do for money?" CB said somberly.

In response, Matt jingled his pockets. "Got them off those uniforms in our backpacks," he said. "Sugihara says they're some kind of subway tokens. They have an image of a reptile on them."

"Look!" CB said. "What's *that* sign?" He pointed to a handbill pasted on a crumbling wall. In front of it an elderly woman was weeping her heart out.

Sugihara translated swiftly: *"By order of the Ministry of Culture. Those desirous of ending their lives honorably because of disappointment in love, career failure, or Zen enlightenment are invited to apply at the Institute for Inner Peace, at the old Matsuzakaya department store on the Ginza.* The rest of it is torn off," he said.

"What could it mean?" Matt asked anxiously.

"I think it means that the traditional custom of ritual suicide has returned to this country . . . with a vengeance!"

Sugihara turned to the old woman. "Why are you weeping?" he asked.

"My husband . . . my children . . . they have sought inner peace," she said. Tomoko could barely understand her through her tears.

"That's terrible!" Tomoko said in Japanese.

"No, Tomoko," Sugihara whispered. "You are only half Japanese. Perhaps you do not understand."

"I understand. From anthropology textbooks, I understand . . . but this is real life," she said.

"What are you guys talking about?" CB said.

"Keep walking," the old man said.

They rode the subway to Meguro station. They found, because Tomoko did not know where else to go, the old anthropological institute. It was boarded up; no servant came to the door.

"It's dark. We've nowhere to sleep," CB protested.

At last someone came. The door creaked open. "Ach, Tomoko." An old voice, a German accent. "Why have you come back here? You have come to hell itself. Who are these people, why did you bring people?"

"Let me in, Professor Schwabauer," Tomoko said. He did so. The house, once splendid, was in tatters. Quickly she introduced the others. "What happened here?"

Schwabauer said, "It was terrible. They came, they took away everybody. For questioning, they said. I haven't seen any of them since. I hid in a linen chest. They kept asking everyone about you, Tomoko. Why? What could they want with you?"

"They want my husband," Tomoko said.

"Oh, it was horrible," Schwabauer said, shuddering. "I never leave the building now. The food is running out."

"It's all right, Professor," Matt said. "We're here to help you."

In the morning they went down to the Ginza. Each carried a small laser pistol, pilfered from the defunct skyfighter, in his clothing. The old man, not wanting to look too conspicuous, had donned a simple business suit.

Long lines of people waited at the front doors of what had once been one of the most chic department stores in Tokyo. "The four of us look too suspicious together," Sugihara said. "Why don't you and CB go and wait in that sushi bar across the street? Because of our physical appearance, I think Tomoko and I will be less conspicuous."

"Right," Matt said. He took CB by the hand and they crossed the street.

The sushi bar sported a pennant on which characters were scrawled. The last had a long, wiggly tail. Matt knew that this was the sign for *sushi,* the delicate concoction of rice and raw fish that was a Japanese specialty. They used to have it at home all the time.

There were two entrances to the restaurant, each covered with a cloth screen. The one to the left said:

The one to the right said:

"What does it mean?" CB said.

Matt shrugged.

"I guess one or the other will do," he said, striding toward the door on the right.

Two burly men barred his path. They wore the costumes of sixteenth century samurai: except that the Visitor logo was blazoned across the material of their uniforms!

"Bijitaa dake!" one of them rasped, pointing to the doorway as if to say, "Can't you read, you illiterate imbecile?"

Matt bowed, the way he'd seen people do in samurai movies, and backed into the other doorway, pulling CB in after him.

Tomoko walked up to the line. A stretch of the sidewalk had been cordoned off to keep the line under control. Grim-faced samurai with Visitor insignia strode back and forth, hands on sword hilts. Each had a glazed look in his eye that Tomoko knew had to be the result of traumatic, total conversion.

"You, there!" One of them shouted at her. "Out of the way!"

"I only—"

"Are you here to seek an honorable death? or are you just here to gawk?" the samurai shouted.

"She is just watching," Sugihara said, covering up for her in case her unidiomatic Japanese might give her away.

"Very well." The samurai turned away to bark at someone else.

"What is it?" Tomoko whispered.

"This is a terrible distortion of *bushido*," Sugihara said. "They've taken the Zen way, so close to their own suppressed *preta-na-ma* faith, and corrupted it into something hideous! Why do they always do this? Your world has a history it . . . a history of killing and maiming in the name of God."

"My world?" said Tomoko. "But aren't you—"

"I mean only the world of Western civilization," Sugihara said, allaying her sudden suspicions.

Suddenly the crowd surged forward. They were rushing to get in! *It's like Friday night at the movies!* thought Tomoko. *Only they're going to die.* The homely image hit her hard. This was what they'd done to her people. They'd transformed the most mundane details of life into grisly parodies of themselves. "I can't watch. What will happen to them?"

"I think . . . I think it is an abattoir," Sugihara said.

"Let's get out of here! I can't stand it! Let's get Matt and the kid and split!"

A huge *shoji* screen separated the two sides of the sushi bar. Matt couldn't see at all what was going on in the other half of the restaurant, the half accessible through the *Bijitaa* entrance.

There weren't any tables. Rather self-consciously, he and CB inched their way forward and sat down at the sushi bar itself. A chef was listlessly slicing a large slab of raw tuna.

"Irasshai, irasshai," he said.

"What?" said Matt.

"Eeto! Igirisu wa hanasu koto ga dekinai no! O-kyaku-sama wa nani o—"

"Excuse me? I really have no idea what you're saying. Just give me some of that." He pointed at the tuna. "Ever had raw fish?" he said to CB as it was placed in front of them.

"Yeah, sure." CB didn't look that pleased. "Right. It's casual." He took a hefty bite. "It's casual," he said, gulping his green tea and looking decidedly out of sorts.

The sushi chef was looking at the boy with his hands on his hips.

"Nice food you got," CB said.

Suddenly they heard a familiar electronic *ping!* "Radical!" CB shouted. "It's 'Galaga'!" He rushed over to the other end of the bar and started to play, relieved to leave the rest of his raw fish still on its board. Matt stared at it for a while (having greedily enjoyed his own) and finally began to nibble on the kid's. Meanwhile he could hear sounds of approbation coming from the corner where CB was playing his video game. He could hear the boy explaining his tricks and someone presumably translating. A universal language, he thought, sighing.

At that point a scream of terror lanced the air.

It came from behind the screen, the other side of the restaurant. The sound was contorted, agonized, yet unmistakably human. "My God," Matt said. "What is it?"

Icy silence fell in the sushi bar.

All one could hear was the quiet *ping! ping!* of the video game and the occasional whoosh of an electronic laser.

Then came the screaming again—

"What's the matter, why won't anyone say anything?"

The sushi chef looked at his feet. The customers all looked away. The screaming went on and on. CB ran to Matt, seeking protection. "What *is* that place? Why are they torturing people?"

"Bijitaa sushi-baa da," said one of the customers.

"Visitor sushi bar? What do you mean . . . I don't know. . . . Oh, God. I know."

"They're eating . . ." CB said.

"We almost went in there!" Matt whispered.

"Let's blow."

"We're supposed to wait for—"

"If we don't we'll be history, Matt. C'mon!" He started to tug Matt away from the bar.

"But I haven't paid yet," Matt said, trying to cover up his fear with mundane details. He tossed a bank note onto the counter (the institute had vast amounts of cash in its safe, which they'd drawn liberally from) and the two of them made for the door. Meanwhile, the groaning went on. . . .

At the door they met Tomoko and Sugihara.

Tomoko said, "It's awful, they're lining up like cattle, they're killing them in there—" Then she stopped. A sharp whining in the stillness: barely human.

Matt looked at his three companions: Tomoko suppressing a scream; CB ghost-pale with terror; Sugihara, his eyes closed, his face composed, lost in a transcendent Zen-like world Matt could never hope to reach.

"CB's right. We've gotta get outa here. I can't listen to much more of this." They slipped out of the sushi bar into the street outside. In the brilliant sunlight, the screaming without was muted: it sounded more and more implausible. Matt understood now how so many of his compatriots had simply refused to believe that the Visitors' intentions could be so evil. It was so much easier to believe the lies. Lies, lies, lies. They surrounded you, they trapped you, and soon you didn't know anything anymore—until you were no wiser than a morsel of raw fish on their dinner table.

Sugihara said, "Do not be angry, Matt Jones. Think of—"

"Vengeance," Matt said.

"—the other martial arts masters, trapped in some terrible hell."

V

"We've got to get into that slaughterhouse," Tomoko said. "And the only way is for me to get in that line." She pointed. Matt saw them then: the crowd zeroing in on the line outside the department store, the cordons, the guards stalking sternly up and down.

"You can't go there," he said.

"I can. Look, I used to go shopping at Matsuzakaya all the time, before they converted it into . . . *that*. They have everyone brainwashed, so they're not going to expect sabotage or spies. There's at least one other way into the department store: the basement level opens out directly into the subway system. I'll go in and do some spying and make it back to meet you at the subway entrance at . . . midnight."

"*I* should go," Matt said.

"No! You don't speak Japanese. Even if you manage to sneak around and spy you won't know what they're saying."

"I should go with her," Sugihara said. "To help fight our way out, if necessary. And you, Matt, you'd better put on your Visitor uniform; maybe you'll be able to bluff your way around with it on. CB will have to be your prisoner or something. See you later."

And the old swordsman and Tomoko went to wait at the end of the line that was endlessly streaming into the house of death. Suddenly Matt said to CB, "The old man doesn't have his sword! And Tomoko—"

"Don't worry, Matt. They're both carrying those little laser pistols concealed under their clothes—remember?"

"Yeah. Yeah."

"Let's go find somewhere where you can change into their uniform." Matt had been carrying it in a satchel slung over his shoulder.

At one end of the Ginza there was, of all places, a McDonald's. The only thing unusual about it was the bathroom, where Matt went to change. It was one of those squatting ones—decidedly un-American! Although the kid was, as usual, enthralled.

When they emerged, people immediately began to make way for him, bowing and looking away with ill-concealed fear. "I guess there are a few advantages to these uniforms," Matt said. "Let's go."

"Oh, Matt, please—"

"What is it now?" Matt demanded.

"Look, dude, I'm absolutely starving and, like, this is the one place where I'm not going to get poisoned with raw fish or something, so, would you mind if—"

The waitress at the counter took one look at Matt in his uniform. They didn't have to pay.

Chapter 15

The crowd moved quickly. It was as if the people in it could not wait to hasten the moment of their death.

Soon Tomoko and Sugihara were admitted into the foyer of the former department store. A few mannequins sported Hanae Mori scarves and elaborate wigs; mostly the shelves were bare. A guard said, "Men to the left; women to the right for disrobing."

Tomoko looked desperately at Sugihara.

Smoothly the old man said, "We have pledged to die together. You see, ours is a double suicide; an adulterous relationship; oh, the shame. You understand."

The guard thought for a moment, then said, "Very well. The two of you may go in together. Down that aisle."

A corridor, a back stairwell . . . the crowd was pushing them along. Doorways on each level, at each a Converted samurai stood on duty, his posture stiff and his demeanor stern.

"All right; let's create a diversion," Sugihara whispered as they neared the fourth or fifth floor.

Tomoko couldn't think what to do. The only thing that sprang to mind . . . unthinking, she started to clutch at her belly, shouting: "I'm going to give birth—" No one could swallow it for a moment, we're doomed, she thought at the back of her mind. The crowd streamed past them, intent on its ritual of self-sacrifice. She went on, wailing and shrieking. A guard rushed down the steps.

"Please help this woman," Sugihara said. "She should face her death with inner tranquillity. . . ."

He and the guard helped her up to the landing. The guard called for another. As soon as the door opened, Sugihara wedged it with his foot, whipped out his laser pistol, and shot the two guards cleanly through. Then he yanked Tomoko through.

"Hurry," he said. "They'll catch on soon."

She looked around. Dark, dark . . . and deathly cold. A medicinal smell in the air. . . .

No! She recognized what kind of place they were in from her captivity aboard the Mother Ship.

Humans hung from the ceiling in neat rows, each one naked, in a slimy, plastic sack. Row upon row. Some were labelled in the Visitors' tongue. Others . . . others had pieces missing.

"Quick!" They heard footsteps. Sugihara said, "We've got to be further into the room."

She could barely breathe for the overpowering stench of meat and chemicals. They ducked into an aisle of bodies . . . were they dead or alive? She could not tell. At the end of the aisle, in jars, were what looked like pickled eyes. She didn't look again.

The steps were coming nearer, nearer; she heard the ringing, metallic saurian speech now, incomprehensible. They retreated behind the body of an enormously fat man. The footsteps were very near now. They were shining a bright light down every aisle.

"Get your laser pistol out," Sugihara whispered.

"I've never killed anyone—"

"Don't think about it. Just do it!"

Lights blinding her eyes! She fired! A brilliant flash of blue laser fire shot through the darkness, she saw serpent flesh split asunder, heard a shriek of pain . . . "They're not even disguised as people," Sugihara said, "they're walking around openly."

"There's more of them."

They retreated just in time. Light flashes in the chamber . . . eerily illuminating human body parts . . . laser light ripping through flesh and plastic . . . "Look," she said, "a gap in the wall. . . ."

"A doorway?"

They slipped inside. Once it had been a stockroom or something; shelves lined the walls. A dim light filtering in from somewhere else . . . from a corridor at the other end.

They heard sounds from the human food locker: more blasts, a collapsing sound as though human bodies had been torn out of their sheaths. . . .

"They're going to find us!" she whispered. "Let's go down that corridor . . . it's the only route."

The corridor was long; it twisted, it opened out onto many other chambers. She remembered how wonderful it had been to buy clothes here . . . on the top floor they'd had—as every Japanese department store did—a whole miniature amusement park with a little merry-go-round, a putt-putt golf course and so on. Before leaving for the Ainu village she'd spent a lot of time here. There now—wasn't that the porcelain section? She peered in. In the shadows she saw nothing but more human beings, carelessly stacked. She quickly went on.

At last the corridor ended in an open doorway.

"Well, what do you think?" she said.

They stepped through.

A wall of *shoji,* the Japanese paper screens that were used in traditional houses, blocked their path. It was well lit from behind; shadowy figures could be seen moving about.

They heard voices . . . the Japanese being spoken was of the courtly variety to be found only in historical movies; Tomoko couldn't understand it all. There were two voices: a man and a woman. The woman's was high-pitched, grating, mocking; the man's obsequious, terror-stricken.

"Poke a hole in the *shoji*," said Sugihara.

"What!"

"No one will notice." He worried at the paper screen with his fingernail until he had worn it a little bare. She did the same. She put her eye to the tiny opening—

And recoiled!

For sitting on a raised dais on the far end of the ornate chamber, dressed in all the finery of an ancient Japanese court lady, was—a reptile! Only once before had she seen such a creature . . . when Fieh Chan had discarded his disguise on the crashing skyfighter. She was heartsick. For she remembered that the sight had stirred in her feelings not only of horror, but of beauty. . . .

She listened to the woman's words.

"That is Murasaki!" Sugihara whispered. "Second in command only to Fieh Chan!"

"How can you tell them apart?" she said wonderingly.

"Believe it."

She listened. . . .

"It has come to my attention," Lady Murasaki was saying to the cringing Ogawa, "that the martial arts project is not going as planned . . . that in the American sector you have bungled several of your abduction attempts! And . . . a Visitor skyfighter was found to have crashed in the outskirts of Tokyo! Answer these charges at once!"

"My Lady . . . I am so ashamed," Ogawa said, hoping that he would not be forced to witness another of Lady Murasaki's bloody feasts.

"Do you realize what this loss means? Until the Mother Ships return, we must nurse our resources as best we can."

"I am sorry, my Lady."

"You'll be more than sorry, fool! I'm sure your ugly head will look a lot better as an ornament to my banquet table than it does on your filthy, scrawny torso."

"My Lady, it would be an . . . honor . . . to die in your service. . . ."

"That's the trouble with you Converted creatures. You don't put up a good fight." Lady Murasaki reared up, shot her tongue out, lashed Ogawa's cheek with it. A dab of venom on his skin . . . he could feel the burning.

A tiny gasp from somewhere in the chamber. "What was that?" Murasaki shouted. "Has someone dared to breach our security?"

"My Lady, that is impossible," Ogawa said, clutching his cheek in pain and desperately searching for an explanation . . . although it sounded quite clearly as if someone were behind the *shoji,* spying. "Perhaps . . . ah, yes, of course, my Lady . . . it's dinner!"

"I suppose it is," Lady Murasaki said, somewhat mollified.

"May I go and have my wounds tended to now?" Ogawa asked humbly.

"I forbid it! Oh, don't worry," the reptile said. "You won't die, yet. I am retreating to the secret hideout at Osaka castle. Wu Piao and the others will meet me there. There we will inspect your handiwork—we will find out for certain whether the martial arts project has proceeded as you say. The dosage I've given you will keep you alive at least a week. Govern Tokyo well in my absence, and I may grant you a dose of antidote. Fail, and—the banquet table!"

"Either one would be an honor," Ogawa said, with heartfelt sincerity.

His reptilian overlord reared up and departed the chamber.

"Now what?" Tomoko said.

"We'd better go. You're the one who knows where the basement exit is, right?"

"Well . . . it *used* to be by the pastry counter on the lowest level, but God knows. . . ."

"That man—Ogawa—is leaving. There's only one way we can—"

Sugihara crashed through the *shoji* and grabbed the Japanese minister from behind. "Your laser!" he rasped under his breath. Tomoko obeyed instantly, pulling out her weapon and shoving it against Ogawa's chest.

"If you scream—" Sugihara said. He made a neck-chopping gesture.

"Lead us out of here. Now," Tomoko said.

"But—but—"

"Stand up tall," Sugihara said. "Like a proper government official. Don't peer around in fright. Have you lost *all* dignity?"

Ogawa's eyes opened wide. "You—you—"

"Ah, you know me," Sugihara said. Tomoko wondered what he meant. "Good. Now, take us to the basement. Immediately."

"Yes."

Tomoko walked beside him. Sugihara walked just behind, his weapon jabbing Ogawa through his suit. They left the chamber. Guards went by; they looked at the three without curiosity. At length they reached an elevator.

They entered. Sugihara did not let go of Ogawa, but continued to cover him with the laser pistol.

Tomoko felt the elevator descending, descending. . . .

"The basement level is disused," Ogawa said. "Possibly you may escape. But please . . . please let me out . . . that I may properly serve the masters . . . or kill me!"

"I will not kill you," said Sugihara. "Once you were a fine man—an able politician, a conoisseur of the arts, generous, warm-hearted. Look at you now!" Listening to him talk, Tomoko realized how little she knew about this mysterious old man who had appeared as if by magic in the shopping plaza in Orange County.

The elevator reached the lowest level. "At least stun me," Ogawa pleaded. "So they won't think—"

"Oh, very well." Sugihara didn't even use his weapon; with his bare hands he found the correct artery in Ogawa's neck, and dealt it a quick squeeze that sent the minister slumping to the floor of the elevator.

Then they stepped out.

They heard the whoosh of the elevator as it returned whence it had come.

Very dim light. Booths and stands, all covered with plastic. "You're the one who used to shop here," Sugihara said. "Lead the way."

Tomoko looked around. "Over there." They eased their way through aisles crammed with crates and plastic. There used to be a stairwell down to the subway . . . there.

They reached it. The metal door, rusty, creaked open.

At that moment, shots rang out. Strands of laser light pierced the gloom. "Quick!" They heard the patter of footsteps . . . then of men stumbling in the half-dark over the crates and boxes.

"Out the door. Heave it shut," Tomoko said.

The two pushed with all their strength. The door would not quite close . . . there was a loose chain. With the heat from his laser weapon Sugihara welded the chain across the door to the hooks in the doorposts. They were getting closer, closer. . . .

Tomoko screamed as a stream of light blasted a hole in the metal of the door, skinning her cheek . . . steps led down, down, down along a tunnel that led, she knew, to a part of the old Ginza subway station . . . what time was it? Her watch read 11:52. Would Matt and CB be waiting at the bottom of the steps?

They ran. From overhead they could hear pounding, pounding . . . then the buzzing of some kind of drill. . . .

Their footsteps echoed in the close, thick air.

Chapter 16

They'd been waiting for almost an hour. The Ginza subway station had been like a labyrinth. By cornering some of the subway passengers, threatening them with his Visitor uniform, and constantly demanding someone who could speak English, Matt was finally able to get a person to direct him through the maze . . . it seemed endless. It reminded him of old movies set in the casbah of Algiers, with its network of dingy passageways. Shopfronts lined the walls, though most were deserted . . . the entrance to the basement of the Matsuzakaya department store was recessed, at the end of a long tunnel, far from the subway platform itself.

Matt had dismissed his guide with what seemed to him to be an arrogant sneer. The role of lizard conqueror was a strangely seductive one, he thought. No wonder so many had become collaborators.

"Time?" CB said.

"Uh . . . about ten minutes till midnight—"

"Look! There they come!"

Shuffling noises from the stairwell. A grating blocked the entryway. Matt could see Tomoko and Sugihara, dim figures, up ahead. He could hear the buzzing of a drill. *How can we open this thing?* he thought. He reached through the grating. No control boxes, no switches. The railings weren't rusty, though; this was obviously a secret way in that the reptiles used all the time.

What could a reptile do that a human couldn't? Of course, they had those long, forked, flickering tongues. . . . Something a Visitor could reach with his tongue . . . he glanced up . . . there it was on the low ceiling of the tunnel . . . a control box with several dimly glowing buttons and switches. He struggled to reach up but couldn't. "If only I could squeeze between the railings," he said.

"I'm small enough."

"Yeah. But you're not tall enough. Here, stand on my shoulder."

He bent down; CB leaped up with the grace of his months of training. He tucked his feet behind the railing. He clung precariously now. Tomoko was halfway down the steps, and they could hear the doorway above crashing and the clang of alien footfalls. "I can't reach!"

"Use your laser pistol!"

The boy was dangling by one arm and Matt was grasping his legs. CB pulled his pistol out and jerked forward. He almost hit the buttons . . . not quite, not quite . . . "They're labeled in lizard speech!" he screamed. "What'll I do?"

"Just hit one!" Matt cried. He felt his hold on the kid almost give way as CB swung forward and bashed the control box with the pistol and—

A second gateway came crashing down from the ceiling, boxing Tomoko and Sugihara in even further! Blue lines of fire hung in the air! Matt heard Tomoko scream as CB lashed out again with the pistol, trying to hit a different button—

The second gateway gave way, retracted into the ceiling . . . Tomoko came running down the steps now . . . Matt could see that Sugihara was grappling hand to hand with a Visitor—no longer wearing a human visage—an alien ninja! With a single swipe of his hand Sugihara felled the alien, who tumbled down the stairs and started to fizzle at Matt's feet.

More of them were rushing down the steps. He saw Sugihara swirling, whirling, and Tomoko was backed up against the front railings now and firing as best she could while CB flailed away at the control box overhead . . . as the alien ninjas were closing in on them, CB suddenly hit another button and—

The gateway shifted upward, pulling up into the ceiling! "Jump!" Matt screamed to CB. He whirled and found himself face to face with a ninja, whom he blasted in the chest.

CB jumped just in the nick of time . . . the gateway slid into the ceiling and he landed on top of a ninja, kicking outward so that the ninja, surprised, toppled and—

"We're all together again. Let's run," Matt shouted. CB climbed out from under the ninja, his T-shirt covered with stains from the ninja's death throes.

They ran. But not before Matt had fired at the control box several times, burning it out. Gateways started to descend at three or four points in the stairway tunnel. He saw one ninja fruitlessly thrusting his tongue up to try to open the gate . . . he burned himself and shrieked a metallic scream of rage.

They ran!

"This is hopeless," he heard Tomoko say. "What've we gained, five minutes?"

He panted, "Don't give up."

They turned down several corridors. Soon they heard the inevitable patter of alien feet again. "We're lost!" said CB.

"No. Wait."

Footsteps echoed and reechoed. Somewhere, the thrum of a passing subway train. "This way." Matt started to go in the direction he thought he'd heard the train.

The four of them sliding gingerly along the walls, finally emerged on a long subway platform. Signs in Japanese pointed in different directions. He could hear a train far away. A light, a long way down the tunnel. Was it coming toward the station?

Too late to think. As Matt looked back up the subway tunnel—

Alien ninjas were leaping out from other passageways. Tomoko shouted, "Look out, Matt!" and fired. A black-garbed assailant fell at his feet. He'd crept up behind Matt. He didn't writhe in agony as the others had when their pressure skins had been punctured. He'd been a human then, a collaborator, a convert.

Matt didn't have time to reflect any further. They were surrounded. And CB was wounded! He ran to cover the kid with his body, warding off the leaping attackers with a barrage of kicks and blows. Sugihara stood above them, serene and still as he picked off the ninjas with chilling precision. Tomoko cowered behind him, emerging now and then to shoot.

"My charge is going," she shouted. "This thing's useless!" She tossed the pistol away. It glanced off the subway rails, sending off showers of electrical sparks.

At that moment the train pulled in and the doors opened—

"Let's go! It's our only chance!" Matt shouted.

Lifting the boy and cradling him in his arms, he ran toward the first open car. Sugihara and Tomoko followed suit. A volley of laser light . . . one of the windows began to melt like butter. Matt looked around. Only a few passengers this late at night. An old man was moaning and drinking from a ceramic bottle of *sake*.

"Come on, close already!" he screamed at the doors. A throwing star whined as it flew through the closing aperture and sheared off part of the old man's face before it spun crazily away and embedded itself in one of the seats.

They pulled out of the station. But when he looked through the end windows and saw the next car down, saw that it was filling up with aliens, he knew that it wasn't over yet. He clutched the kid tight. CB was bleeding profusely, but it seemed to be only a superficial arm wound, it would be all right if he could fix it up soon . . . and started to move forward . . . they forced the door open and stepped into the next car. A single ninja was there waiting for them. Sugihara disposed of him with an instant burst of blue flame.

"That seems to be the last charge," he said.

He tossed it away.

"They're coming!" They train barreled through a station. "They're not going to stop!" Matt exclaimed. "This isn't one of the regular trains."

"No, I guess not," Sugihara said ruefully. "These things don't have drivers. They're computer controlled from a central terminal. They could be taking us anywhere for all we know."

"Oh, God," Tomoko said.

"Come on. Let's force our way to the front. Maybe there's a control panel or something one of us can jimmy," said Matt.

They pushed forward. The aliens were following. Matt handed his and CB's laser pistols—the only ones still working—to Tomoko and Sugihara. The two of them covered while Matt, still sheltering CB in his arms, moved forward. On the very front car, in a glass booth, was a console of some kind. . . .

CB stirred. "Let me take a look at that," he whispered, almost inaudible.

"Hold still, kid."

"No, let me look at it. If I can whip 'Galaga,' I can whip any low-IQ computer on a subway car."

Matt broke the glass. CB clambered in. Pulling a video game token out of his pocket he began methodically to unscrew one of the panels with his uninjured arm.

"Just as I thought!" Matt had to strain to hear him. "Look at this!" He pointed to a green board in which were embedded a number of microprocessor chips.

"Are you okay, CB?" Tomoko said.

The ninjas were only one car away now. They could hear
the scuffling; they could hear the shrieks of the car's few
passengers as the aliens shoved them out of the way.

"Tomoko and I will lie in wait on either side of the door,"
Sugihara said. "Matt, you cover the boy."

Matt looked ahead. He saw long lines of bright dots on
either side. In the far distance they divided. "Must be a
fork."

"Here we go," CB said. He started to tug the microchips
out of their sockets. Then he yanked the whole board out
and tossed it aside.

"Need help?" Matt said, although he had no idea what
CB had just done.

"Hell no, I'm jamming now." He sat up and began to
peruse the Japanese-language labels on the console. "Wish
I understood this stuff," he said. He closed his eyes. "Eeny
meeny miny mo, here goes!"

"Cut us loose!" Matt screamed at Sugihara. A spidery
figure in black had succeeded in forcing open the door;
Sugihara dealt it a blow over the head. Another came. They
kept coming and coming. "Cut the car loose!" Matt
screamed again.

Tomoko began to fire at the latches that yoked the two
cars . . . fire broke out between the cars, the aliens'
bodies caught fire, their ninja garments exploded in foun-
tains of flame and clouds of foul-smelling vapors.

"I'm going to hit the button now," said CB. "I'm not
sure what it'll do, but—"

He did so.

They swerved! The connection between the cars ripped
asunder . . . they shot to the right with a ninja trailing out
the door, while the rest of the subway train vanished down
the left fork. . . .

"What happened?" Tomoko said.

"Our kid appears to be a computer whiz," Matt said,
panting heavily.

"Once you've licked 'Galaga' . . ." CB said. Then
exhaustion overcame him and he passed out.

"Can you read any of this stuff?" Matt said to Sugihara.

"Let me see . . ." said the old man, stepping over the shards of broken glass that had sealed off the control console. "Ah, yes. The brake. That might be useful."

"Our ordeal isn't over yet," Tomoko reminded them. "The anthropological institute is near Meguro station; you can't get there on this subway system, you have to change at Shibuya for the Yamanote line . . . you can't even do it by controlling the car on manual; they don't even interconnect, it's a different guage or something."

"Is that Shibuya ahead of us?" Matt said. Indeed it was. Sugihara hit the brake and Matt could read the sign clearly now, for it had English beneath the inscription in ideographs.

They careened to a screeching halt.

Crossed the platform, climbed up to the Yamanote level.

A train stood waiting on the platform.

"It's dead," Matt said.

CB, stirring in his arms, said, "Are we there yet?"

"There's a train, but I think this line has closed down for the night, I think it's just parked."

"Let me at it!" CB said. "You seen one controller board, you've seen 'em all."

CB dismantled the train's remote controls with ease. As they pulled away, with Sugihara watching over the console, Tomoko began to bind CB's wounds, tearing strips off her own dress.

"That feels good," CB whispered.

"Always wanted a kid," she said, half to Matt, half to herself.

"Meguro, here we come," Sugihara said.

CB said, "I'm much better now. Thanks."

They pulled in.

Then they left the train, exited the deserted station, entered the square, and started walking toward the institute. . . .

But . . . something was wrong! The sky flickered, red and yellow. A blast of hot air from the direction of the institute.

They were running again.

As they reached the alley—

Fire! The buildings beside the institute, built like so many Japanese houses only of wood and paper, were in flames; the institute itself was smouldering, already reduced to ashes. The highrises that had towered above the institute now had balconies extruding tongues of flame. Men and women were rushing about madly, many of them weeping. This was so much like the day of liberation, Tomoko thought . . . the crowds running wild, congesting the alleys, tumultuous and wild. But then it had been elation that so moved them . . . now it was. . . .

She stopped a man. "What is the matter?" she shouted at him.

"Don't you know anything? They came for the *gaijin* martial arts master . . . they said he was hiding in the institute . . . then they burned it down . . . they're hunting people down, devouring them in the streets. . . ." He ran away, cowering at the sight of Matt's uniform.

"There goes my beauty rest," Tomoko said grimly. Nobody laughed. They made their way through the press of humanity to the institute itself. Ashes, nothing but ashes.

"Our belongings. . ." Matt said. "The rest of the stuff we stole from the skyfighter . . ."

Tomoko watched as Sugihara strode into the center of what had been the main downstairs room of the institute. He was wading knee-deep in ashes; they were not quite cool yet, for she noticed that he winced once or twice. He bent over, plucked something out—it looked like a broken chairleg or something—and seemed to be digging around in the ashes with it. At last he found what he was looking for.

It was a sword.

He picked it up. Its hilt was charred; but the blade shone, golden-red, against the burning highrises overhead. He held it up, high, high, high; it flashed brilliantly, like a setting sun.

"The bastards," Matt whispered, looking around him in dismay. "What have they done to Rod and Lex and Kunio? Where have they taken them?"

"To Osaka Castle!" Sugihara said.

"Why?" CB said. "I've seen that castle on TV—it's a famous monument."

"Something is going on there," Tomoko said. "Something horrible."

"Well," said Matt, "I've come this far. I've been in this place for maybe twenty-four hours and I've seen that they really are after me—enough to kill innocent people—enough to risk *their* lives too. I don't know what it is, but I don't like it, and I'm going to fight them to the end, the bitter end!"

"That's my dad," CB said, his eyes shining.

Tomoko came close to the two of them. She embraced them both. This tiny moment of love was precious to all of them, she knew, because they were so surrounded, so trapped. . . .

Still Sugihara stood. His tranquillity was deceptive; she knew that every muscle in his body was tensed and ready for any sudden attack.

Suddenly he broke his pose. "You will go to Osaka Castle, then?" he said. "You will risk . . . everything?"

"Yes," Matt said fiercely.

"Good." Sugihara regarded the three of them with an expression of almost Buddha-like beneficence. "There is much good in you, Matt Jones," he went on. Tomoko noticed a certain wistfulness in his voice, as though he were longing for something that could never be. "You have a fine wife and child. And all of you have left your homes behind to come with me, even though you did not know me, even though you did not entirely trust me . . . I know that you have wondered what I am, Matt Jones. I must tell you more now. I am not what I seem—"

"You're—"

"No. I am not one of your enemies, Matt Jones. Come. We can stay here no longer, obviously. Haven't you even wondered whether I have a home here in Tokyo? Have you wondered whether there is still a resistance movement here, now that the country seems entirely run by Converted people and collaborators, its economy and technology in shambles, its people disheartened and helpless? It is time to answer those questions now, Matt Jones. . . ."

Chapter 17

Sugihara led the way. Down alleys choked with smoke from the burning institute. Apart from the main thoroughfares, Tokyo has no street names; addresses are given in terms of so-and-so district, such-and-such turning, so many houses down the lane. Tomoko had no idea where they were going, though it seemed that their path led downhill. The little street was coiled like a serpent; in the dark they could barely see, but Sugihara seemed to know every step of the way from memory. They walked swiftly, not seeming at all exhausted from the gruelling chase in the subway system. CB sometimes walked, sometimes was carried. A lugubrious Professor Schwabauer took up the rear. They hardly spoke.

At length they reached what seemed to be a restaurant or tea-room; it was at any rate completely shuttered, unlit. A lone penant hung from the doorway, scrawled in calligraphy of such refined elegance that Tomoko was unsure of its meaning.

Sugihara went around to the back; he tapped gently on a side window. A woman came around to open the front door and admit them. To Tomoko's surprise, she was dressed in the full regalia of a geisha; her face was painted white as the moonlight; her mouth was brilliant carmine; her hair neatly coiffed and bunned and set off by a silken hair ornament. *"Doozo sumimasen,"* she said, bowing to them and pointing out a place where they could remove their shoes. The Americans, with varying degrees of awkwardness, imitated Sugihara, who did all the polite things as smoothly as might a cat. They stepped onto a raised *tatami* floor and sat on the floor around a tea table. Without any fuss, the geisha began to pour steaming tea into bowls.

A look passed between her and Sugihara. Tomoko felt a quick flash of . . . could it be envy? Theirs was a tradition of centuries, a tradition she ought to understand and be in tune with but . . . instead she was forever torn between her two identities.

"I should explain," Sugihara said to the others. "In Japan it is considered unthinkable for someone in my position not to have a little house of retreat somewhere to which he can flee from the troubles of the world, and find solace in the arms of a mistress. But Setsuko here is no ordinary geisha . . . she is also a scientist."

"UCLA," the geisha said, bowing reverently to the assembled company, "doctor's degree in astrophysics, master's in chemistry and biochemistry. I am sorry to seem to boast."

She'd been to America, then, this woman, had an American education . . . how could she have ended up like this? Tomoko couldn't help saying, "A Ph.D from UCLA and you're this unliberated?"

"We all seek different things in life, Tomoko-san," she said. "Knowledge was not everything to me. I also needed inner discipline. So I have come here, received some training in my second calling, and found myself mistress to the great Sugihara himself."

The great Sugihara, Tomoko thought. There is a lot more to the old man than I ever imagined. Who was he really?

Setsuko listened gravely while the others recounted all the events of the day. Then she said, "Osaka Castle . . . that will be difficult. You say, then, that the Visitors are walking around openly as reptiles? That they no longer masquerade in their artificial skins?"

"That seems to be true," Tomoko said. "And with such men as Ogawa having been Converted, and everything that might remotely be construed as anti-saurian removed and replaced by pro-lizard platitudes—as an anthropologist I can easily see how, in only a generation, all the negative images associated in the culture with reptiles could be plucked out . . . it's as though they were performing a kind of surgical operation on the collective brain of an entire society!"

"*Hai*," said Setsuko. "And the answer lies in Osaka Castle."

"To think that you actually came face to face with Fieh Chan—the creature who engineered this whole thing," Matt said angrily to her. "To think that he almost . . . touched you. . . ."

"It does not sound to me like the work of Fieh Chan," Setsuko said. "All those who knew him for any length of time discovered that . . . beneath his horrifying, reptilian exterior . . . there was an inner core of compassion."

"It's true," said Tomoko, "that he saved my life." She did not want to say that she had felt . . . attracted to him. She didn't want to hurt Matt's feelings.

Setsuko said, "You will help us?"

"Yes," Matt said.

"Yes," said Tomoko and the kid.

Setsuko said, "We are so unfortunate compared to you in America. Our young men expended so much energy in the *kamikaze* attacks on the alien institutions; reprisals were swift and terrible. Our resistance was utterly crushed during the period of alien rule. But our hearts still burned! We thought we had been liberated . . . but no. Though humans ostensibly rule us, their minds are possessed by Conversion; and Fieh Chan's thermal pressure skins have enabled many of the saurians to remain here! But if they were dispossessed of their stronghold, how long could they last? I think the people would rise up. They cannot fight a real war without their full weaponry, without their Mother

Ships. They have perhaps two or three skyfighters down here on earth. We could have killed them all, but we lacked the will; our souls had been stolen from us."

Tomoko was deeply moved by her impassioned speech. She realized that she had never been attached to one land, one tradition the way Setsuko had been. Part of her longed to be like Setsuko; another part yearned to be fully American.

"But I've been working on something in my laboratory," Setsuko said, "that I think would help."

She clapped her hands.

The shoji behind them were drawn aside. Beyond, Tomoko could see . . . rows of gleaming test-tubes and retorts and flasks and reagents and Bunsen burners. A lab assistant in a white coat smiled to them.

"I've analyzed the dermoplast samples from a number of Visitor disguises . . . and I've been able to reproduce it. It's a strange substance, not quite plastic, not quite organic. Like living tissue, its production involves cloning." Setsuko's assistant brought in a little lacquer tray; with a fluorish he lifted the piece of silk that covered it.

It was wrinkled, green, scaly . . . but Tomoko saw at once that if it were stretched taut it would look exactly like the face of one of the Visitors. "It's astonishing," she said.

"It's not that good yet," Setsuko said, lifting the dermoplast and pulling it between her fingers so that it resembled the webbing of ducks' feet, "but I think that, in dim light, it will pass, no? Why not? I mean, they fooled *us* with this stuff for quite a while."

"But what use is this?" Matt asked.

"I think that the only way a small number of people can penetrate Osaka Castle is to turn the tables on them . . . to disguise ourselves as reptiles," said Setsuko.

"What? Wear lizard masks?" said Matt.

"More than just masks," Setsuko said. "The entire body is, ideally, to be covered. Of course, we don't have time to do that; we'll have to do the best we can."

"Are you telling me that just the four or five of us are going to storm an entire castle wearing Halloween costumes?" Matt said incredulously.

"It's our only hope," Sugihara said. "Murasaki has already left for the castle . . . something is brewing. We don't have much time."

"Okay," Matt said. "I'll buy that. But tell me one thing . . . why were they after *me* in the first place? I mean, why was a bunch of aliens in Japan trying to capture martial arts masters from America in the first place? They have plenty of them here, don't they? And what would they use them for?"

"This is my theory," Setsuko said. "You see, their position is much weaker than it seems. Sure, they're controlling the country via their Converted puppets . . . but they're not much in contact with their Mother Ships, if at all, right? If they're running low on weapons, they wouldn't be able to get that much locally; Japan's armed forces, because of the post-Second World War treaties, are minimal. They'd have to go native all the way. But several months ago, many of the leading grand masters in this country committed mass seppuku."

"They killed themselves?" CB said.

"No one quite knew why."

"Among them was my own teacher, the great Sugihara," Sugihara said. "That is why I have taken his name for my own. . . ."

"And his mistress," Setsuko said, bowing deeply. Tomoko saw how proud she was, and she felt a strange envy. She would never understand this woman.

And if Sugihara was not Sugihara, who was he?

"It seems to me," said Setsuko, "that perhaps the aliens are involved in a mass training program. They don't know when the Mother Ships will return, if at all. They must think they will—otherwise why all the food processing plants, thinly disguised as centers for honorable suicide? They must be, as it were, going native, learning the local martial arts techniques as a safeguard for the day that their technology is depleted . . . the grand masters of Japan, in all honor, could not participate in such a thing, and so committed *hara-kiri*. So they've been abducting them from other countries. . . ."

"And they're holding them all in the castle?" Matt said.

"Probably in Conversion chambers," CB said grimly.

"You're right," Matt said. "If we can fool them long enough to get inside, we can probably free our friends and there's probably some way we can sabotage the whole installation—"

"But what about the voices?" Tomoko asked, remembering with a shudder the first time she had heard their harsh tongue, when she was frozen in the plastic sack in the food lockers of the Mother Ship. "And the language—we can't learn the language in time."

"I have a device that may help; it's similar to ones used by cancer patients who have had laryngectomies. They are held against the throat, and they produce a buzzy, raspy voice quality . . . I've adapted it a bit. All the masks will be equipped with one."

"But the language itself—" Matt said.

"We'll just have to use the old alibi that it's official policy to practice the terrestrial languages at all times, even out of earshot of humans," Tomoko said, remembering her captivity.

"Seems pretty risky to me," said Matt.

"Let me at their central computer!" CB said enthusiastically.

"I don't know if you should even come with us," Matt said. "You don't need this, kid, you've been through so much already—"

"Hey, they ate my 'rents. I'm gonna kill them. We're Batman and Robin, remember?"

"Yeah," said Matt. Tomoko saw how much love they shared, her husband and the kid, and she was glad she had found him again, glad of his newfound gentleness. Yet there was something about Sugihara too . . . she remembered her father, always shouting and complaining about her mother speaking Japanese in the house and about heathen ways . . . she had always fantasized about a lover who would also be a different kind of father . . . Asian like her mother . . . more forgiving.

Two men—two ways of life—Tomoko was afraid to choose.

Chapter 18

While Tomoko, Sugihara and the others slept, Matt and CB wandered down into the basement of Setsuko's laboratory. They found Setsuko and a couple of assistants hard at work—of all things, painting a car bright orange.

"What is this?" Matt said. Looking around, he saw that he was in a garage. There was an entranceway out onto the street, heavily barred; probably an alleyway.

Setsuko looked up. "Not asleep, Matt Jones?" she said. "You have a hard day ahead of you."

"But what are you doing?"

"Oh, camouflage, you might call it. You have to get to Osaka castle somehow, don't you? And only the aliens are allowed to ride around in cars and to obtain gas from gas stations. Here, help me with this."

She took out a stencil, taped it over the car door, and began to spray black paint on it. It was the hated symbol of the Visitors, so similar to the Nazi swastika. "I have to drive in this?" he said.

"I'm sorry," she said.

"Spare me."

"I have much else to do tonight. I also have to see about your wardrobe. I think it's best for all of you to be dressed very inconspicuously, no? Ninja outfits. They're working feverishly on all your disguises now. Do you want to see?"

She led them to a back room where an old woman was at work painting masks. The dermoplast was stretched taut over the Styrofoam heads used in wig shops; and the old woman was carefully drawing in every scale. "My grandmother," she said, introducing them and murmuring a few words in Japanese.

The old woman looked up and uttered a long string of breathless syllables.

"She says that she thanks you for volunteering to give your lives for the sake of the future," said Setsuko.

"None too reassuring," Matt replied.

"Can I try one on?" CB asked.

He spent the next hour or so looking like a reptile and grimacing into a mirror.

"How can you be so calm?" Tomoko said to Sugihara, who was sitting in a meditative pose, his sword in front of him, his eyes closed.

Sugihara said, "I have learned much."

"I envy you," Tomoko said. "I—"

"You need not hold it back, Tomoko. By tomorrow night we may be dead."

She told him the story of her life. Only to Fieh Chan, she recalled with a chill, had she ever been this candid. "What will I do if I see him again?" she said. "Fieh Chan, I mean. There was something about him . . . you have a bit of that something too."

"Be happy, my child," Sugihara said. "I am much farther from home than you."

What did he mean by that? "You must have suffered a lot," Tomoko said.

"Yes."

She didn't know what to say; Always he unnerved her by his directness. This directness, she suspected, must conceal great complexity. It was as though everything he said hovered on the verge of truth, and yet was not quite true. She couldn't stand the silence, though. She had to make conversation. "Ah . . . do you believe in reincarnation?" she said, picking a random cocktail party subject in her nervousness.

"I have already lived many lives, I think," Sugihara said. "Indeed, I am not the person I have been."

"You're such a mystery. Your sword is beautiful. Is it hundreds of years old?" She touched the carved hilt, admiring its smoothness.

"It belonged to my master. To the last, he did not know my true nature," Sugihara said.

"What is your true nature?"

"I don't know."

I don't either, she thought. "Did he mean a great deal to you? The master Sugihara I mean, the man whose name you've taken."

"Yes. We were very close. He commanded me to be his second in the act of *seppuku.*"

Tomoko trembled. She knew what that meant. The second in *seppuku* was always a trusted friend or comrade of the man who was committing suicide. It was his duty to decapitate his friend as soon as he had completed the act of ritual disemboweling. It was dreadful to contemplate.

"I could not follow him, Tomoko," said Sugihara. "For he commanded me to go on living."

"Is that so awful?"

"More than that. I had to compel myself to go on living . . . because of a memory."

"Whose?"

"A woman." Sugihara stared straight into her eyes. She wished so much that she could do something to comfort this strange, incomprehensible old man. Impulsively, she kissed him on the cheek. His skin was cold, deathly cold. "The woman was much like you, Tomoko Jones. How lucky your husband is."

"Sometimes I don't think he appreciates me."

"He does. I see it. He is not a thinking man; he doesn't articulate his feelings. But you've seen how he has changed."

"Yes. Yes," Tomoko said, weeping passionately.

Chapter 19

The limousine stopped to refuel at one of the few operating gas stations on the highway, halfway between Tokyo and Osaka. It was painted orange and its doors bore the ominous Visitor sigil. Lady Murasaki stepped out for a moment, for she did not relish traveling in such primitive vehicles. Hours it had taken them to come even this far; and the roads, uncared for since the breakdown of technology, had been unpleasantly bumpy. How she longed for one of the desert hoverskimmers on the home planet! Or even the silk-smooth whisper-quiet flight of a skyfighter.

A lackey—one of the converted creatures—came out to service the vehicle.

"Gasoline situation?" She spoke harshly, as one must to lower creatures.

"Very little left, my lady," said the attendant. "I fear there is only enough for a few more tankfuls. If in your mercy you should be able to procure more . . ."

"There is no more," Lady Murasaki said petulantly. "But the masters will soon be returning."

"Of course, my lady."

She walked inside the building.

Within, there was a battered coin-operated Coke machine that in its better days proffered canned peach juice as well as carbonated drinks. It no longer worked. A lamp that exuded the odd odor of some kind of fish oil burned on the desk;

electricity, then, was no longer known in this rural area. Of course they had had to divert the entire production of the area's one functional power plant to the castle; a delicate, experimental filtering device was at work there to cleanse the atmosphere within the compound of the red dust, but it was not effective enough. Fieh Chan's confounded pressure skins were still needed even within the castle itself. What a nuisance!

Murasaki sat down at the desk and drew a small communicating device from a fold of her kimono. It was about the size of a personal stereo; a small flat screen was blinking.

"Ah, Wu Piao," she hissed. "You've been trying to reach me all day?"

The face of her colleague and sometime rival appeared, tiny in the viewscreen. "Murasaki! Good. Communications have been even worse than usual. Or is it simply that you do not choose to respond to urgent calls from your colleagues?"

"I trust you are on your way to Osaka, Wu Piao? Or haven't you left Hong Kong yet?"

"Since you have assured me that Fieh Chan is returning, I am accepting your invitation to come and inspect your facility." Clearly he knew that his choice of words would infuriate her. "I am anxious to receive my orders from the one most qualified to give them," he added pointedly. His voice sounded tinny on the machine's miniature speaker; Murasaki wished heartily that it were always so small, like a buzzing fly that one could flick out of the air with one's tongue and swallow. "I am taking our only skyfighter, Murasaki. I trust you will not allow it to be destroyed? You have been most wanton with skyfighters, and they're not, at present, replaceable, as you well know."

"Sabotage somewhere in America can hardly be attributable to me," Murasaki said.

"The destruction of the skyfighters means, Murasaki, that someone knows something they're not supposed to know! An information leak! I thought that all your servants were converts?"

"Any problem will be dealt with in my own inimitable fashion," Murasaki said coldly.

"Yes. We all know about your human sushi bars!" said Wu Piao, chuckling. "The one thing you do well, my dear—thinking up new ways to serve dinner."

That reminded her. She was so hungry . . . that gas attendant now, perhaps . . . no, just a snack was what she needed. She looked around. Ah, a rat. There it was, perched on the edge of the desk. She stared at it, hypnotizing it with her gaze. Then, with deft and deadly precision, she shot out her tongue, sprayed it with venom, toyed with it while it wriggled for a few moments; then popped it into her mouth.

"Must you always eat when I'm trying to have a serious discussion?" Wu Piao said.

Ignoring that remark, she continued, "I hope you will arrive in time for dinner. We have a wonderful surprise planned."

"To see our leader will be enough," Wu Piao said, not even bothering to camouflage his insincerity.

So he doesn't believe me! Murasaki thought. *Well! By tomorrow he won't be around to doubt. I shall eliminate him, and with Fieh Chan out of the way, with all the processed food ready for export, with the newly trained corps of martial arts fighters firmly in control of Japan, there's no question about who's going to be in charge of this whole forsaken planet!*

She sat at the desk, laughing uproariously to herself at the prospect of being the next great leader.

Presently, she became aware that the gas attendant had entered and was watching, waiting for an opportunity to speak.

"Well, you idiot?" she said. "What is it?"

"My lady, earlier today another Visitor limousine passed this way. A message was left for you."

"Well, out with it!"

He pulled a piece of rice paper from his shirt pocket. On it, in delicate calligraphy, were the words:

BEWARE
THE ALIEN SWORDMASTER
IS COMING

"What is this?" she said. "Who gave you this?"

"I did not see his face, my lady. He was garbed as a ninja."

"He came here? You gave him gasoline? But none of the other masters is scheduled to travel this road today. If you have betrayed me—"

"Oh, no, my lady! I saw his eyes. He was a master, I've no doubt about it," said the attendant in terror.

A sliver of doubt penetrated her thoughts. But she would not allow it to cloud her mind. After all, Osaka Castle was impregnable.

Chapter 20

The first time Matt had looked up at the mirror when they pulled out onto the road, he'd scared himself.

"Those faces are certainly convincing," he had said. "The woman does good work."

"She is a good woman," Sugihara said. "It is almost a pity to leave her behind. But if we do not return . . . someone must remain to try to hold together the fragile threads of the resistance."

They drove on.

None of the traffic lights worked. Matt drove furiously, as though possessed. In a way he was possessed. He had to prove something to Tomoko. He'd seen the soulful stares she and Sugihara had been giving each other. He wasn't going to lose her again. No way.

"You're supposed to drive on the left, Matt, this is Japan," Tomoko said to him as they roared up the Shuto Expressway.

"What difference does it make?" Matt had said, and continued to drive on the wrong side of the road. No one stopped him. Children and vendors ran screaming as he approached. "Now I know how Godzilla feels," he said. "I'm glad I'm human."

Three lizard faces stared back at him.

Matt felt awkward. He was by far the tallest of them; CB, tall for a twelve-year-old, completedly swathed in the black vestments of a ninja, was as imposing as the other two, but Matt felt gangly and out of place.

"I hope Professor Schwabauer's all right," Tomoko said. They'd left him behind at Setsuko's house.

"Sure," he said, wondering whether they would return to find that house, too, in ruins. "He'll be all right."

They drove on.

At length, after stopping to refuel at one of the few working gas stations on the highway, they had reached the environs of the Castle just before nightfall.

"It's beautiful!" said Tomoko.

Indeed it was. It reared up at the summit of a hill, from its bed of lush vegetation, a thing of pointed eaves and walls within walls and stone staircases with carved balustrades.

"But it conceals a terrible sickness," Sugihara said.

At the foot of the hill they reached a barricade.

A guard waved them on.

They reached a second and a third one. At the third one, someone came down to talk to Matt. It was an alien; the ridged forehead and cruel eyes were visible through the black garments.

He barked out a string of Japanese, which Matt couldn't understand at all. "He says he doesn't seem to know us," he heard Tomoko whisper.

"What'll I do?" he whispered back.

Sugihara said something back to the Visitor guard.

The guard bowed instantly and opened up the barricade.

"What did you tell him?" said Matt.

"That his superior officer would hear about this!" said Sugihara.

Within the compound, there seemed to be a lot of activity. Matt pulled into the parking lot. A number of orange cars, some of them limousines, were there. "An extraordinary amount going on," Sugihara said, "considering what things are usually like here. . . ."

"How would you know?" Matt said.

"I have been . . . in captivity before."

There were steep, walled steps carved into the hillside. Above them, the castle was silhouetted in the setting sun.

"Never show any fear or hesitation," Sugihara said. "The Visitors delight in finding fault; they will jump on the slightest error. But they hate to admit they're wrong, and if we can bluff them, we're in. Now, are your throat synthesizers in place?"

"Yes!" said Matt, testing it out. The voice that issued forth from the device startled him at first; it was terrifying, tinged with metal.

"Right. Let's go," Tomoko said.

They left the car and began to walk up the steps.

At length they reached an imposing archway of wood. Guards stood on either side; they were humans, converted.

When they saw the four of them they immediately bowed; one of them made to lead them up the last few steps into the castle gates. Sugihara and the guard exchanged words; Matt saw a strange expression on Tomoko's face. He dropped behind and asked her what they had been saying.

Tomoko said: "The guard said, 'Welcome; I presume you're here for the meeting? Let me show you to your quarters.'"

"They were expecting us?" Matt said.

"I don't know anything more," Tomoko said. "They seem quite certain that we're supposed to be here. In fact, we're supposed to appear at a banquet in our honor . . . in a couple of hours!"

"Oh, no," CB said. "I bet I know who the main course is."

PART FOUR

OSAKA: THE ALIEN SWORDMASTER

Chapter 21

"Very well," Lady Murasaki said to her guardsmen, "I suppose I'd better inspect the prisoners before dinner."

They escorted her down the corridors of the castle. It always thrilled her to see her personal guard, with their samurai uniforms made of cloth blazoned with the Visitor insignia, each holding aloft a banner. Though this was a dreadful world in most things, it certainly had a great deal of barbaric pomp and splendor. She intended to keep the spectacle after she came to power. That much she knew for certain. She was certain, too, that after tonight's banquet she would hold all the strings of power in her own hands.

Unless Fieh Chan had somehow not only survived, but had also gotten wind of this whole situation. That was the only fly in the ointment. But Murasaki, as she strode proudly down the hallways with their floors of polished wood, slippery against her scaly, shoeless feet, was supremely confident that her moment of triumph was at hand.

"I shall visit the conversion chambers first," she announced.

"Yes, my lady," said a guardsman. One was a saurian, the other a converted human. They slid open the *shoji* panels into a large chamber in which, in a cubicle surrounded by complex apparatus that radiated an eerie blue glow, a man hung in chains. He was naked, and electrodes were attached all over his body.

"Ah," she said coldly, "Mr. Casilli."

Rod Casilli looked up. "So you're back, you reptile," he said. "You think you're going to turn me into one of those mindless morons, I suppose! Well, it'll never work. I'll resist you—resist you—resist you!"

"But why bother, my fine friend from America?" she said in a grotesque parody of a coquettish, cajoling tone. "All your colleagues have already capitulated. Your friend Lex Nakashima has already joined my army. He is already involved in the training of thousands of cadres. The sooner you give in, the sooner you'll be able to get back to that nice estate in New Mexico. We'll even give you that electrified fence you wanted so much. It's not so bad, being one of us, is it? At least you'll be on the winning side."

"Any master of martial arts will tell you that winning is not the issue!" Rod groaned.

"Very well. As you insist," she said. To the guardsman: "Initiate phase two of the conversion."

Jagged bolts of blue lightning streaked across the cubicle! Rod Casilli twitched and jerked about as though jolted by electric charges. His eyes began to bulge from their sockets. Sweat poured down his cheeks, his neck, his well-muscled torso. Animal screams tore from his throat.

"Enjoying yourself, Mr. Casilli?" said Lady Murasaki, licking her lizard lips with her forked tongue. "The machines are very patient, I assure you. And so am I. Infinitely patient. Mr. Ogawa, the minister of culture, didn't crack for several weeks; but what a loyal subject he is today! Why, today he reported to me that he was regretfully forced to eliminate a friend of yours. Jones, I believe the name was—Matt Jones."

"Matt—you bastards! You killed Matt? But I just talked to him before you captured me, before you brought me out here. He called to warn me. It's terrible that I didn't believe him. To think that I laughed off that telegram about the alien swordmaster."

"Alien swordmaster?" Murasaki was temporarily startled out of her complacency, for she had been unable to solve the riddle of the message she had received that afternoon at the service station. "What do you know of an alien swordmaster? Speak! Or I'll be forced to continue the torture!"

"I don't know anything!" Rod Casilli screamed, as Murasaki reached out with her flexible tongue, prodded the dials of the conversion device to turn them up higher.

"By the time I'm through with you," she grated, "your brains will be so addled you really *won't* know anything! Except what *I* choose to implant there."

To her satisfaction, she noted the pain index and read the brainwave indicators of the apparatus. A feisty one, this! But it was always so much more gratifying when they broke. Like training an intractable beast. "Come, come," she said seductively. "See with our eyes. You need not suffer so. You can be happy, happy . . . let me melt away your resistance . . . it is making you unhappy. . . ."

"You killed Matt Jones!" Rod shrieked.

"Yes," Murasaki said, allowing a tone of hypocritical regret to enter her voice. She hoped Jones really was dead, that Ogawa's report had not been its usual mishmash of hogwash and bungling. The man had been so intelligent once, but there was no doubt the conversion process took away some of these creatures' reasoning abilities; they became like children; you couldn't rely on them to do any job that required *thinking*.

"Continue the process," she instructed the guards, "until he cracks."

"Lady Murasaki, I don't think the poor thing can take much more. . . ."

"I don't care! Reduce his brains to jelly if you must! What does one of these martial arts masters matter? We have so many of them in our power already."

"Of course, my lady," said the guard, bending down to operate the machinery while Murasaki turned away, intent on continuing her inspection of her pet project.

"Where will you go next?" the other guardsman—the human—asked.

"Oh, the dungeons, I think," she said. "I'll have a little chat with Nakashima and Yasutake and Kippax."

"I'm afraid, my lady, that Kippax has died. The—ah— conversion process proved too much for him."

"But the others?"

"Dealt with as you commanded."

"Good. I'll go down and see them, and . . . then I'll inspect the training grounds themselves; we'll want a nice display of power, won't we? To impress the delegates from Hong Kong, Seoul, and the other places. After all, we must show our future vassals who's going to be boss. Afterwards I shall go down to the kitchens and discuss the banquet menu with the cook. I'll want nothing but the best for our seven delegations."

"Seven, *tono*? I heard from the gate guardsmen that there are eight, Lady Murasaki. Another delegation, comprising four members, turned up just before dusk."

"Oh? I wonder who they are?" Lady Murasaki said. A tiny sliver of dread pierced her thoughts, but she made herself ignore it.

No, she thought, *nothing must cloud my hour of triumph—nothing!*

Chapter 22

"No," Sugihara said, "I don't think we *are* going to be the main course after all. We seem to have arrived at a very dramatic juncture in the Visitors' constant political power struggles. I think that Lady Murasaki intends to try something tonight, something really big."

"She wants to dispossess Fieh Chan himself?" Tomoko said.

"Perhaps so," Sugihara said.

They had been shown into a chamber of astonishing elegance. Four futon beds had been neatly arranged on the tatami floor. A balcony looked out on to an inner courtyard of the castle, which was at present empty. A low table held a tea service and a silver platter of neatly arranged appetizers. The food was red and bloody, and Tomoko didn't want to imagine what it might be.

"Well," Matt said, "what's the plan? Obviously CB and I can't go to dinner. They'll be talking Japanese—or maybe this lizard talk—and I don't think I'll be able to fake it. Besides, I think I should snoop around some. I want to look for Rod and Lex and anyone else they might be holding here . . . and find out why!"

"You're right," Sugihara said. "Let's see . . . we have about two hours to cook up a plan."

At that moment they heard noises coming from the courtyard. Lights flashed. "Let's go look," Tomoko said.

They went to the balcony.

Floodlights were being set up. Tomoko saw a saurian wearing an elaborate kimono, and she recognized that it was Lady Murasaki.

Presently a long line of youths began to file into the courtyard. All wore orange headbands on which were blazoned the Visitor symbol and all wore training suits in the same ominous colors. Lady Murasaki regarded them, unmoving; her eyes seemed to glitter. They arranged themselves in lines. They bowed to her with militaristic precision, their simultaneous footfalls resonating hollowly on the smooth flagstones of the courtyard.

Lady Murasaki nodded.

At that moment a man entered the courtyard. He was gray-haired; he walked like a zombie; the life seemed to have gone out of his eyes. He wore the same uniform as the youths. As Tomoko looked at each of them, she saw that they all had the same lifeless eyes. There were boys as well as girls; some were as young as CB, some seemed to be in their teens or early twenties.

The Lady Murasaki nodded again.

This time they all gave a great cry, sharp and fierce. It echoed around the courtyard and faded. Then they sang an anthem. She couldn't make out all the words, but they were in praise of the Visitors . . . and of Lady Murasaki in particular.

She was sickened, but she watched on, terrified and fascinated.

"It's like a whole army of zombies," she whispered, awed. "An army of people who have lost their souls."

A man came up and gave a few shouted, harsh commands.

"Oh, Jesus," Matt said suddenly. "That's . . . that's Kunio Yasutake!"

"The grand master of *takodo*?" Sugihara said. "You're sure it's him?"

"Of course I'm sure. He told me on the phone that

Ogawa had done him the honor of inviting him to Japan for a special demonstration of his rare art. I guess he didn't know he'd be training a bunch of killer zombies!"

"He's been converted," CB said grimly. "Like I remember, that's how Sean Donovan looked."

"What are we going to do?" Tomoko said.

Below, in the courtyard, the youths commenced to practice. They moved smoothly, menacingly, all together, in a slow ballet of violence, aping Yasutake exactly.

Lady Murasaki called for them to stop. They did so immediately and stood to attention, their eyes fixed on her. She progressed up and down the lines. Always her eyes glittered. Was it lust? thought Tomoko, remembering Fieh Chan. Or was it hunger? She couldn't tell. Presently she stopped and pointed to one of the youths—a boy no older than CB.

Trembling, the youth stepped forward.

Lady Murasaki clapped her hands again.

Yasutake's voice sounded in the vast courtyard. "Today I will demonstrate another type of killing move. Watch, observe, obey."

"We watch! Observe! Obey!" the army chorused.

For the first time, Tomoko saw, fear seemed to enter the boy's face. "I obey," he said. His voice was almost inaudible.

Then, setting his face into a mask of concentration, he readied himself, froze into the formal stance of *takodo*. For a long moment nothing happened. Then the boy seemed to explode in a whirl of energy. He rushed toward Yasutake, a war cry shrilling from his childish throat.

Yasutake stood, his arms half outstretched, wrists and elbows curved inward. His arms seemed to have no bones at all, to imitate exactly the arms of the octopus, from which his particular martial art took its name. When the boy leapt up to attack him, Yasutake, without seeming to exert himself at all, made a waving motion with his arms, drew the boy in. It all happened almost instantly. All you heard was a small cracking sound. For a moment Tomoko did not realize that the child's neck had been snapped.

"Demonstration over," Yasutake cried. "Now—you will all practice the following moves—"

"I think I'm going to be sick," Tomoko said.

"This is not the way," Sugihara said, shaking his head sadly. "These arts are sacred. They were not meant for the mindless slaughter of innocents! Self-defense is one thing, but systematic killing just for demonstrative purposes . . ."

"I see Murasaki's plan," Matt said. "This is her contingency for when the laser guns run out of power. She plans to rule, with or without the Mother Ships! By training an army without a soul—an army that won't hesitate to immolate itself at her whim—an army of total converts."

"We gotta stop them," CB said. "I don't know how, but we gotta."

"Well," Matt said, "since CB and I don't speak the language, I guess our job will be to sneak around and see if we can dig up our friends."

"And Tomoko and I will go to the banquet and try to see exactly what is involved in this newest power game. Ah," Sugihara said as someone tapped lightly on the *shoji*, "someone has come to summon us."

A servant came in and bowed.

Tomoko said, "What do you want?" trying to sound authoritative, utilizing her synthesizing voicebox.

The servant said, "Lady Murasaki has asked me to ascertain exactly which delegation you belong to. And how many will actually be attending the celebratory banquet."

Tomoko felt a mild sense of panic. Had the disguise slipped for a moment? She ran her hand over her face, feeling, through her reptilian gloves, the hand-etched scales and mottlings that Setsuko's grandmother had so painstakingly created on the dermoplast mask.

She didn't say anything. Sugihara came to the rescue. "You will tell the Lady Murasaki," he said, "that we are extra members of the Seoul delegation who have decided to appear at the last minute. Moreover, you will stop questioning us—or I will see to it that you end up on the banqueting table yourself! However, to satisfy your catering arrangements, I should inform you that only two of us will be coming to the dinner. Those two"—he pointed to Matt and CB—"are clearly of inferior rank." He spoke as though the servant were a fool for not realizing these facts immediately.

The attendant, cowed, bowed abjectly and said, "Of course, master. I am so sorry. It is hard at times for us miserable creatures to tell you masters apart—"

"We all look alike, eh?" Sugihara said in a tone of barely concealed menace.

"I didn't mean—master, if I offend—"

The servant backed out of the room, bowing all the way.

"Now that we're alone again," Sugihara said, "let me explain something of the geography of the castle to you, Matt. The dungeons are located . . . over there." He pointed past the courtyard to a tiny entranceway.

"How do you know so much about the castle?" Matt asked.

"I told you. I was imprisoned here once. The conversion chambers are in the vicinity of the dungeons. You'll just have to explore. Now the banqueting hall . . ." Sugihara described the complex path of stairways and corridors they would have to follow to reach it. "The banquet hall has a number of secret passageways. One, behind the dais from which the shogun used to hold court, leads directly to the rooftop on which the skyfighters are usually parked. Behind one of the movable walls there is a computer complex which operates the entire castle; most of the electricity in this district has been diverted to run it and its subsidiary functions. Now you will attempt to find and release the grand masters—those who haven't been converted—and enlist them in our cause. Meanwhile, *we'll* go to the banquet. We'll learn all we can about what's going on. I get the impression that most of the lizard honchos—those that are still knocking around this part of the world, who haven't fled in the Mother Ships—will be at the banquet. They'll be busy dividing Earth into three parts, if I know them, anticipating what'll happen when the Mother Ships return. You and your friends, Matt, will interrupt the meeting, and then . . . well, that's where my plan sort of peters out. I suppose we shall improvise from there."

"Improvise?" Matt said.

"In the absence of any more information, that's all we can do. Maybe we can sabotage their computer or something."

"I'll do some serious hacking," said CB.

"Precisely," Sugihara said.

"I'm afraid," Tomoko said. "I don't want to confront Fieh Chan once more. He confused me so much."

"We all have something within us that we don't want to face," Sugihara said. "May you have the courage to face it and conquer it."

"May we all," Matt said fervently.

The sounds of combat came once more from outside. Matt went to look; he saw that Kunio Yasutake was demonstrating his skills to another group now. Lady Murasaki had left.

"He was a good man," Matt said. "Now he's as good as dead. I'm never going to be like that. I'm going to die fighting. Like Anne did. When I look at the man down there . . . I see his body but I don't see him, I only see a shell, a husk. They want the whole world to be like that, don't they?"

"Have you heard of *preta-na-ma*?" Sugihara asked.

"No."

"It means 'peace' in their language. They were not always like this, Matt. Believe me. They have a terrible sickness in their souls. But . . . but there is good in them."

"Try telling that to the kid out there, the one whose bones old Kunio crunched up!" Matt said.

"Or my mom," CB added.

"Listen. Throughout history there have been periods when intolerance ruled, when humans—sentient beings—persecuted, enslaved other beings just as sentient. Look at the witch burnings! The Inquisition! Look at the Nazi holocaust! Was that any less cruel than this? And yet the human race is a compassionate race. And because it knows compassion in the fullest sense, it must know also the dark side of compassion . . . do you know what Anne Frank said in her diary? *'Ich glaube an das Gute in den Menschen.'* 'I believe in the good in men.' We all know what happened to her. . . ."

"You're a very educated man," Matt said. Though at first he had felt nothing but envy for Sugihara, he had finally developed a grudging respect for this infinitely patient, Zenlike old man. "You sure know a lot about history and stuff. I know only one thing—those lizards are taking away my freedom, and I'm going to fight to the death to keep it. For me—for my wife—for my kid."

"Right on, Matt," CB said admiringly.

"I only want to point out to you that the Visitors have, in their suppressed ancient religion of *preta-na-ma*, something as beautiful as the Zen philosophy. I dream of the day when we can live in peace with them. Think of how much we have to give each other!"

"Pipe dreams, old man," Matt said. "Me, I hate to think. Maybe that's why Tomoko left me in the first place, huh?"

"She has come back to you," said Sugihara. "Things will get better, I know it."

"Now, don't go putting words in her mouth. But Tomoko, I want you to know that whatever you decide is okay by me. I made that decision when I saw the way you sit at Sugihara's feet and drink up his words. They're good words, I guess. I won't stand in your way. I used to be selfish, but I've learned that that's not the way . . . to love people."

He looked at Tomoko. There were tears in her eyes. They flowed out onto the mask, past the yellow alien eyes, onto the rubbery-textured imitation skin. "Don't cry," he whispered. "You'll smudge the paint job Setsuko's grandmother did."

She wept even more. Did she truly love him? He could not tell. He knew that in the vast struggle between man and alien this relationship was less important than freedom. And if he was going to fight for freedom he had to be willing to accept Tomoko's freedom too. Whatever the consequences.

They decided that Tomoko, who of the three of them knew no martial arts, should have the last of the laser weapons that still carried a charge. It was a hand-sized blaster, and she tucked it easily into a fold of her dress.

Then the four of them put a few finishing touches on their Visitor disguises and parted; Sugihara and Tomoko to await the summons to the great banquet, CB and Matt to raid the dungeons of Osaka Castle.

Chapter 23

The guests were beginning to file into the banquet chamber, which Murasaki had arranged in traditional Japanese style. A single, long, low table to accommodate the couple of dozen guests. Silken cushions, stuffed with rose leaves and embroidered with the Visitor symbols, were placed around the table. Murasaki herself was to sit at the head of the table, in front of the dais and the enormous folding screen that concealed the entrance to the central computer console of the entire castle complex.

She saw Wu Piao and hastened to greet him, making sure that she used just the right tone of condescension.

"Ah, there you are," she said. "I've awaited your arrival with anticipation."

"How nice, Lady Murasaki," Wu Piao said testily. "But you promised me that Fieh Chan would address this gathering personally, and I see him nowhere! Furthermore, every one of the guests I've talked to has been wondering about the same thing." He furrowed his scaly brow expressively, and his tongue darted out to flick down a passing dragonfly. "Beat you to it," he said. "I was always faster than you, even when we were students at the war academy together."

"You do ill to remind me of our misspent youth," Murasaki said. "Especially since our positions will soon be so vastly different as to be unable to brook any of this camaraderie. . . ."

"Ha! Expecting promotion, are you, after tonight?" Wu Piao said, plopping himself down on one of the soft pillows.

"Quiet, Wu Piao. If you are good, I may permit you to rise rapidly through the ranks—for example, if your sexual favors pleased me."

"I see you've gone native far more than you'd like to think, Murasaki my dear. I believe you've fallen prey to what these earth creatures call the 'casting couch' mentality."

"Take care, Wu Piao!" Murasaki hissed, and sat down rather ungracefully upon her cushion.

Something odd caught her attention. "Look at those two!" she said, pointing to the pair who sat at the opposite end of the table, one in male, the other in female attire. "There is something remarkably sallow about their complexions. Don't you think their scales seem to be peeling, or sagging, or something? Who are they, anyway?"

"I don't recognize them," Wu Piao said, after scrutinizing the two, who were conversing quietly to themselves, and not at all participating in the raucous conversation of the others. "They certainly seem a little weird. I thought you had handled all the invitations yourself. Didn't you?"

"Well, indeed, but there was also a clause, if you recall, issuing a general invitation to any other Visitor VIPs who were stranded here and could make it to Osaka Castle on time. I wanted this to be a victory celebration, not to leave anyone out by accident who might take it amiss and—"

"End up sabotaging your wily schemes, Murasaki! I know you of old. It's like their fairy tale of the evil fairy who wasn't invited to the castle. Ah, but you haven't made as much of a study of their culture as I have. Crude, fascinating stuff—extraordinary, sometimes, how it seems to provide a distorted mimicry of our superior culture."

The hors d'oeuvres were being set before the guests now. There was a kind of gelatinized broth containing swimming amphibians, and a chilled blood cocktail; nothing fancy, Murasaki noted, but prepared to perfection. Those chefs she had converted had certainly become adept at preparing what the masters wanted. . . .

"You know," she remarked, scrutinizing the dinner guests once more, "the more I look at them, the odder they seem. Do you notice, for instance, how strangely they're staring at the food? How insulting! They act almost disdainful of it . . . and they're hardly touching it."

"Be charitable," said Wu Piao. "You have so much to rejoice about, have you not?"

"I suppose you could say that," Murasaki said. But she continued to watch the two strangers curiously. Something was not quite right about them. For a moment she suspected some machination of Fieh Chan—but that was impossible! Not tonight, not the night of her brilliant, rigged revelation!

Lady Murasaki clapped her hands for silence. "Announcement time," she said.

Scaly faces turned toward the head of the table.

"I have great revelations for all of you," Murasaki said. "First, let us talk about the thermal pressure skins that we are all wearing at the moment. They will soon no longer be needed."

A chorus of consternation ran through the assembled diners.

"Our studies have shown that in some parts of this planet the toxic level is actually decreasing. It has been statistically determined that this is most likely to occur in areas that do not have harsh winters. This means that we will soon be able to declare parts of the planet open to colonization again, that the Mother Ships will return, that my warehouses full of processed food will soon be emptied of their contents. I shall earn the undying respect of those above me in our hierarchy—and be properly positioned to seize the next available rung in the ladder!"

There was some scattered applause.

"But we don't know how long it will be before the

Mother Ships return. Meanwhile—for now at least—our weapons resources are dwindling. But doubtless you've been hearing about the training of my new troops. I call them the army without souls."

"Wonderful, wonderful!" she heard someone shouting.

"I have asked my armies to provide a couple of volunteers for tonight's entertainment."

The *shoji* were drawn aside, revealing two sleek young men, well-oiled. They stepped out and bowed smartly to Lady Murasaki. Guards laid out mats on the tatami; the two men waited in opposite corners.

"These are two of our young converts," Murasaki said. "They will fight for the privilege of *not* being the main course tonight. Is that not a delicious concept? And they will be demonstrating some of the new skills their teachers have been imparting to them, teachers imported at great expense from as far away as America! But before they fight, one final revelation. A moment of sadness."

She clapped her hands once more. A wailing, dirgelike music welled up from a *gagaku* music ensemble: screeching woodwinds and fifes, pounding drums. Some of Murasaki's converted servants came in, bearing aloft a tray on which rested a small jade urn. They set the urn down beside her; reverently she lifted it up.

"Alas," she said, "this is sad news indeed." Her tone did not seem to carry much melancholy, however. "As all of you know, on the day that the red dust first reached this region of the planet, we were not that well prepared. Many died. Those to whom the pressure skins could be distributed in time survived, of course. I wish I could say the same of our glorious leader, Fieh Chan, who after all was the inventor of this device that has enabled us to retain our toehold on this world. But Fieh Chan was not to witness his own triumph. I did not wish to announce his sad death before for fear of panicking my people; I wanted to wait until we had a firm power base once more. This urn contains all that is left of him . . . almost unidentifiable, after the red dust gnawed away at him and destroyed him utterly."

A moment of stunned silence. She could see the astonished look on Wu Piao's face, and could scarcely contain her delight. What a brilliant stunt she had pulled! Pressing her advantage, she continued, "Of course, I had to wait until all you important survivors were gathered in one place because I want to make absolutely certain that no one questions my right to take over the supreme command of the Osaka Castle–controlled sector of our empire!"

The guests were looking at each other now. She took pleasure in their confusion. Her glance wandered swiftly from one to the next. They were simply too astonished to speak. *How stupid they are!* she thought. *Almost as moronic as human beings*. At length one of them reluctantly shouted out the words "Long live Murasaki, our new commander!"

Another and another took up the cry. There was not much enthusiasm, Murasaki noted, but she remembered, as she gave the signal for the two young men to begin their combat, what an ancient Earth tyrant had once said: "Let them hate, so long as they fear!"

Chapter 24

"Quiet!" CB whispered. "We don't want to wake up the whole neighborhood, right?"

"No . . . well, we're supposed to, though. We're supposed to go around as if we own the place. I think that's the idea." Stay calm, Matt told himself, sweltering under the dark garments; it was a close, humid evening. "These aliens' home planet . . . do I get the feeling it's hotter than ours?"

"Guess so. Or they'd fix the air conditioning. Phew!"

"This way, I think Sugihara said to go. Left."

They passed bamboo-lined corridors. Guards, listless, waved them on. "The dungeons . . . they're just down there," Matt said. "Look, one of those doorways that lifts up from the floor." He swaggered up to the guard and pointed imperiously at the door, thinking, I might as well go out in style.

Instead the guard merely flicked a switch; the doorway was raised; Matt saw worn wooden steps leading into the dank, musty spaces beneath.

And moaning . . . and . . . was that the clanking of chains?

"I feel like I'm in a horror movie," CB said.

"Easy now."

They went forward. At every turn they saw the brutalized Converts that made up Lady Murasaki's army without

162

souls . . . all of them, seeing what they thought were masters walking among them, fell prostrate, pulled piteously at their chains to try and reach their lords' feet, called out their praises in broken voices. Though Matt could not understand what they were saying, their tone was unmistakable, and he was sickened by it.

"Hey, Matt, look at this!" CB's excitement was almost uncontrollable. "Look, in this room here. . . ."

Matt caught up to his apprentice. Looked inside. There was a man hitched to some diabolical device that emitted flashes of blue flames and jags of lightning, on which dials spun madly and switches were lit up. . . . "I know that man," Matt said, "although . . . I've never seen him so broken down, so defeated . . . he looks like he's the middle of some incredible nightmare."

The man twisted his body taut against the restraints, shouted out "Never! Never!" and seemed to faint.

"He's speaking English!" CB exclaimed.

"It's Rod . . . Rod Casilli," said Matt. "Oh, no . . . I hope it's not too late . . ."

Rod looked up; saw the two of them standing in the doorway. "So you're back," he said, his voice barely audible. "You've come to torture me again . . . but I'm never going to give in, never! Especially since I've found out what you did to Matt!"

Matt went up closer. Gathering what little energy that was left to him, Rod managed to rear up and spit into his face.

"Hey, come on, man," Matt said. "You're messing up my disguise—"

"Here they come," CB said. "Quick! Back into lizard mode!"

"Hurry up, Rod, feed me some lines—I don't know what I'm supposed to be doing here!" Matt said heatedly as they heard the thud of alien boots in the hallway outside.

Rod seemed very confused. Then he finally said, "I won't give in! You'll never convert me, never! I won't train your army without souls. I'd rather die."

"Figures," said CB. "It's a conversion chamber. Well, first, let's unplug these electrodes," he said, reaching up and yanking some wires from Rod's body.

"Hey, careful! How do you know it's not some kind of life-support mechanism?"

"Oh, Matt . . . have I ever steered you wrong before?"

"Matt . . . is it really you? . . . But . . . you're wearing . . . you look like one of *them!*" gasped Rod.

"No time to explain now. Go on protesting!"

Rod continued to groan and scream imprecations.

The guards paused behind Matt and CB. Clearly they didn't understand English. But they were egging Matt on. CB continued to operate the dial even though it wasn't wired to anything anymore, occasionally emmitted what Matt thought were extremely convincing sadistic shrieks.

One of the guards barked something incomprehensible at him. This was the moment of truth! Matt turned to face him, turned his throat device on as loud as he could, and said, "I'm one of the English-trained personnel, specially brought in to question these American prisoners. If possible, could you let me perform my task in the officially assigned language?"

The guard looked curiously at them both, then shrugged. A second one, who seemed to know a smattering of English, said, "Your appearance is strange."

The first guard suddenly noticed that the electrodes weren't attached to the martial arts master in the machine. He pointed to it angrily, and began berating CB for incompetence.

"Here goes nothing!" CB cried as he delivered a flying kick at the alien's jaws. The other one, mystified, lumbered forward to see what the fuss was, when Rod disentangled himself from the remaining wires and leaped on top of him. The commotion had stirred up some guards from outside now. They could hear clanking and clattering from all directions. The guard whom CB had downed was now getting up and rubbing his head. Swiftly Matt moved to put him out of action again.

"This way!" Rod said, pointing to a narrow passageway just behind the Conversion device.

"But that leads farther into the building. . . ."CB said.

"Well, it's better than going out and fighting a couple of hundred angry saurians, isn't it? Come on. God, I feel like the Frankenstein monster," he said, rubbing himself and peeling off a few more wires, some of which still dangled from his limbs and torso.

"Right then. Let's go," Matt said.

They crept into the passageway. As they entered, Rod took a small folding screen from the wall and stopped up the entrance with it. "This is how Murasaki used to come in to question me," he said hoarsely. Water dripped down either side of the passage . . . barely more than a crawlspace. Soon they saw windows on either side opening out over more dungeons . . . this was, then, some kind of inspection passage, a vantage point from which, doubtless, jaded Visitors could come down and watch the torture and mayhem . . . Matt saw their lightless eyes, their wan expressions, and he knew they had all been Converted, all, all . . . did they plan to do this to all Japan? To the whole world, if the Mother Ships should ever return?

"Listen," Rod said. "They're behind us."

"They can only come single file, though."

"Look . . . there's more people we know!" CB hollered, pointing through the grating at what seemed to be Lex Nakashima and Kunio Yasutake.

"Okay." Matt listened. "They're coming from both directions. CB, get in the middle and try to unfasten this grating."

"Yes, Matt."

Matt could see one of them now as he turned his back on his old friend Rod. Only the eyes were clearly visible, for they were wearing the ubiquitous ninja uniforms that so many of these Visitors seemed to favor; they burned like red hot embers in the darkness. Grabbing a piece of piping overhead, Matt lifted himself, positioned himself as though for a giant swing, and rammed into the alien's face with his feet. He felt the lizard collide with those behind him, heard the whoosh of escaping gases that signified the collapse of the saurian's protective pressure skin. Another clambered forth over the seething corpse of his predecessor. Matt ducked a blow, spun around to trip the alien only to find himself face to face with another who had breached Rod's defense—"Take care of him for me!" Rod yelled. Matt despatched him with a blow to the neck. "Only if you get *this* one," he said, as the one he'd been trying to catch managed to crawl under his feet and was clawing the air in Rod's direction. Matt didn't have time to watch what Rod would do . . . he had his hands full again as several more ninjas came dashing down the passageway.

"It's open!" CB yelled triumphantly, as the grating dropped with a fearful clang down to the stone floor beneath and prisoners scrambled to get out of the way.

"Jump!" Matt yelled.

All three of them did so. The prisoners, thinking CB and Matt were the lizard overlords, began fawning over them.

"These guys are converted, right?" Matt said. "They'll do anything I say."

"That's the idea," Rod said.

"I think I got a plan." He called out brusquely to the assembled prisoners. "Now which of you speaks English?" he said, using his voicebox for maximum effect.

"I do, master." said one . . . God, it was Yasutake! And Yasutake didn't even recognize him.

"Listen. Those aliens up there are bad, do you hear? They're . . . they're in revolt against the proper . . . the proper ethics of the saurian community. We are on our way to report this whole shocking plot to Lady Murasaki at the banquet. In the meantime, you must fend them off until help comes—kill them if necessary!"

"But—they are masters too—"

"Obey!" said Matt in so chilling a tone of voice that even CB jumped out of his skin.

"Not bad role-playing, dude," CB whispered, shaken.

"Here they come." The ninjas pursuers, having ascertained that the three had jumped, were following suit now, leaping one by one into the chamber.

Some of the prisoners were milling about confusedly as Yasutake started to explain Matt's "orders" to them. Many were so perplexed they did nothing at all . . . but some were convinced. They began to close in on the attackers, methodical, almost somnambulistic in their motions.

"We'd better duck out here before they catch us," Rod said. "I can't believe that used to be our friend . . . well," he said, as they entered an empty corridor at the end of which there seemed to be stairs back up to ground level, "I think it's about time you told me what the *hell* you're doing here in that ridiculous reptile makeup!"

The sounds of scuffling from inside that dungeon cell were not incredibly comforting as Matt tersely related the entire tale to Rod from their last, desperate phone conversation to that moment. "And now," he finished, "Sugihara and Tomoko are sitting up there in the lizard's maw, just waiting to be discovered. . . ."

"Wait—did you say Sugihara? The great swordmaster Kenzo Sugihara? He's dead . . . I heard he committed suicide."

"Yes, I know," Matt said. "This is a pupil of his . . . who took his name."

"Sugihara had no pupils," Rod said. "That's why not that many people knew about him. But he did have one, it was rumored . . . one of the high-ups in the lizard hierarchy! You don't suppose—"

"No. It can't be," Matt said. But this was the secret fear that had tormented him the whole time. "Oh, God. It's not true."

"I didn't say it was. Besides, this fellow has helped you, hasn't he?"

"But they're devious."

"Sometimes you're a little too xenophobic, Matt Jones. But come on, we'd better go to the rescue. And we'd better get us an army first."

"An army?" CB said.

"Sure. We'll go into all the prison cells . . . we'll tell them the same story . . . about the bad revolutionary aliens who are a threat to our cause. Right? Hell, with that disguise and that voice contraption you look and act so mean your own mother'd kill you. When people have been brainwashed they're very suggestible, and if you can come across sounding vaguely like the swill they've been getting from their lizard masters, we've got it made."

"And the guards?"

"I think we can cope with a few guards," Rod said grimly. "I've been meaning to show them a few tricks of *ikakujitsu* for some time.

"Okay. Let's go. One, two, three dungeon cells between us and the stairway. You think I can talk them all into it?" said Matt.

"Give it a shot," Rod said. "It's all we can do."

They went into the first chamber. There were no guards at all; apparently they felt that the converted ones were so safe they could be left alone! That was their greatest failing, these lizard folk from the stars, Matt thought; they were blinded by their sense of superiority, unable to credit humans with any kind of ingenuity at all.

They saw him and prostrated themselves as was required. Then Matt began speaking, in English, while one of them translated to the others. Matt was thinking: *Deep down in these people's hearts there's got to be a place these monsters haven't touched. They don't dare admit it to themselves . . . for fear of this self-punishing mechanism that the alien brainwashing will induce . . . but they want to do it, they really want to. If I can phrase it just right, if I can make it really sound like the lizard masters. . . .*

Was it working? "I command you! Help me rid our

empire of these dissidents. Let them see that our might is irresistable!" *God, I'm sounding like an old movie villain,* he thought. *But maybe, considering the pulp these lizards have left in these guys' heads, maybe it's about the right level to aim at. . . .*

One by one the converted began to fall into line. Some, driven practically schizoid by the contrary pull of their conditioning, were pacing back and forth, trying to puzzle it out. But others had enthusiastically launched into a blood-curdling chant and were pulling out bamboo swords and other practice weapons, all that they had available.

"Follow! Follow!" Matt shouted, as he made his way to the next cell and the next—

And finally emerged in the central courtyard of the castle . . . at the head of a bewildered but bloodthirsty army!

Chapter 25

"They've noticed us. I'm *sure* they've noticed us!" Tomoko whispered to Sugihara. "What was she just talking about anyway?"

"She says that that urn contains the remains of Fieh Chan," Sugihara said, as the reptile at the head of the table continued to orate in her screeching voice. Food continued to be brought in, appetizers and small things Tomoko did not care to look at too closely; instead she looked behind her, out of the enormous bay window from which extended a small parapet.

"Do you think it's true?"

"I can't say," Sugihara said.

Tomoko continued to sit rather uncomfortably. "Look. Why are they staring at us?" she asked suddenly. "Don't we look right or something? I don't know how long I can keep this up."

"It's all right. Now . . . hold the gag reflex. I think they're bringing on the main coarse."

She heard the raucous hooting that passed for laughter among these creatures . . . an enormous platter was being wheeled into the room, a platter whose contents smelled suspiciously like . . . roast pork . . . pork, pork, where was it she'd heard the expression 'long pig'? Wasn't it in the first anthropology class she'd ever taken, when the subject of cannibalism came up and Professor Schwabauer told the students, his jowls shaking, that 'long pig' was what they called human flesh in some parts of the world? That it was considered the greatest delicacy amongst many races? She knew she shouldn't be shocked, she should keep a cool analytical mind, she should just imagine that she was doing some kind of advanced field work disguised as an alien, infiltrating their culture . . . as they bought it to the table, her senses reeled. She struggled to quell the nausea . . . at some level knowing too that the smell was not unpleasant, was even . . . delicious. . . .

The saurian to her right said something to her; she responded in Japanese. "Oh? You have a fancy to practice one of the outlandish human tongues?" he said. He was an older creature; his cheeks seemed to sag, and the scales seemed to have lost their shine. "Very well. I'm getting a little rusty myself, and it will of course still be necessary to deal with the nasty things even after the return of the Mother Ships."

"Ah," said Tomoko, pretending to nod sagely.

Just then, the covered dish was wheeled in their direction. "You'll love this," said the saurian. "They always try to choose a specimen suitable to the occasion, and in this case. . . ."

The dish cover was lifted.

She knew this man! His name was Kippax, Jonathan Kippax. He'd been one of Matt's best friends, and was supposed to have been in on that ill-fated tournament. It was too much for her. She couldn't help it. A shrill scream escaped her lips.

They all turned around to look at her.

"Now the fat's in the fire!" Sugihara said coolly. "You'd better be ready to—"

At that moment—

Rattling sounds from the courtyard outside! Resounding footsteps . . . shouts of *banzai* and terrifying warchants.

An attendant rushed in and threw himself at Murasaki's

feet. "They're attacking, My Lady, I don't know why, they're attacking—"

"What! I ordered no late-night demonstration. That was to have been tomorrow!" Murasaki cried out in ire, pulling a little flail out of her kimono and laying into the unfortunate servant. "Tell them to stop immediately, do you hear? Immediately! Or you'll be dessert tonight!"

"*Tono*, they are not demonstrating, they are actually attacking *you!* They're on their way up to the banqueting hall—"

"What impertinence! How can they possibly be attacking us? They're converted creatures . . . not only subreptile but actually subhuman!" With a disgusted flick of her tongue she daubed the attendant's face with venom and left her, lying howling on the tatami floor.

Murasaki ran to the window to look. The other guests, ignoring their food, rushed over and began to crowd each other . . . their oppressive odor pervaded her nostrils, a stench of fetid, carnivorous breath and scaly dryness. "It's true!" Murasaki said. "Call in my ninjas at once!"

Alarms blared through the castle. Lights flashed from the courtyard beneath. Tomoko saw the Lady Murasaki standing at the window, looking out over the parapet. Murasaki was resplendent in her glittering, many-colored kimono; her squamose face seemed to shine in the lights that strobed up from the flagstoned court beneath. As Tomoko pressed closer to watch, she saw a small troop of crack ninjas leap down from windows, roofs and balconies. A volley of arrows burst into the artificially lit night.

Marching out of the dungeons . . . wasn't that Matt, CB and . . . Rod Casilli? How many of the other captured martial arts experts had they rescued? Behind them marched the armies of converts, and Tomoko saw from their eyes that they had not been liberated.

As arrows raced towards them Matt reached up and grabbed their shafts in his hands, his teeth, plucking them in sheaves from the air . . . an ancient ninja trick Tomoko

had never seen in real life before. Then his army ran
forward and began hand-to-hand combat with Murasaki's
ninjas.

She was right behind Murasaki now, elbows practically
touching. . . .

"Now!" Sugihara shouted in English. "Get her!"

Tomoko pulled the laser pistol from a fold of her kimono
and shoved it hard into the small of Murasaki's back.

Murasaki shouted something incomprehensible.

"Listen to me," Tomoko said harshly. "Away from the
window. Against the wall." Louder, she said to the others,
"You others, against the walls." Sugihara had pulled out
his sword and his laser pistol and was motioning the aliens
into a corner and covering them.

In a fury, Murasaki screamed: "What is this? Insurrection
in the ranks of my own subordinates? How do you think the
High Command is going to look at this? I told you the
Mother Ships were returning!"

They could hear the thunder of footsteps now, as some of
the rebels were breaking through the ninjas into their wing
of the castle.

"You underestimate us, Murasaki. You call us animals.
You use us as servants. You feed on us. Yet—" and, making
sure her pistol was trained on Murasaki, she carefully
peeled off her mask with the other hand.

The lizards recoiled in horror.

Suddenly, Murasaki's hands broke through the *shoji* of
the wall and hit a gong on the other side. It boomed.
Tomoko fired in panic . . . her wrist seemed to give way,
she just couldn't do it at point-blank range . . . scaly
hands seized hers and held them fast, pain wrenched at her
shoulders. She was being held by two lizard ninjas who had
leapt in through the paper wall.

"Now, you with the samurai sword. Drop it at once
. . . or the woman dies and is added forthwith to our
repast," Murasaki said coldly.

"Don't do it!" Tomoko screamed.

"I will not!" Sugihara said. "For I have information that you need, Murasaki. Information without which your empire will forever be incomplete . . . information without which your quota of pressure skins will never be filled and the number of Visitors will gradually be thinned out by death!"

"You have nothing for me. Especially if you are . . . one of these disguised mortals. You shall be killed and eaten along with her."

"I have information," Sugihara continued quietly, "that you have feared for months, Murasaki . . . that you have tried to ignore. It's no use. You are not in command here. *I* am!"

He tore the mask from his face.

It wasn't the face of Kenzo Sugihara!

"Yes, Tomoko," he said slowly. "I am sorry that it was necessary to conceal my identity from you. I did not think you would accept my help otherwise. . . ."

Tomoko said, bitterly, "What will you do now? Kill us all? Now that we've helped you recover your own authority? Will you attempt to have your way with me again?"

"No," said the alien swordmaster. He spoke very gravely, in measured tones. He was much as Tomoko had remembered him, months before, when they had had those few hours together, when she had poured out her heart to him, a stranger, an alien. To think that she had harbored him in her own home! That they had travelled together unknowing all this time . . . that she had never once suspected—

Yes. She had suspected. She had even hoped. . . .

"And now," Fieh Chan said to Lady Murasaki, "what am I to do about you?"

Chapter 26

As the aliens stared about uncertainly at this astonishing turn of events, Fieh Chan continued to speak: "Release the woman! Now!" As they did so, Tomoko recovered her laser pistol. "Now, Tomoko, keep these people backed against the wall. Come with me." Carefully he stepped up onto the dais beyond the head of the dinner table. "Soon Matt Jones and his fighters will reach this banquet hall."

"The outcome is far from as certain as you seem to suggest!" Murasaki screeched.

"It is indeed!" said Fieh Chan. "Let me tell you something. Isn't it true that for the past four months you have been desperately searching for the key to the Castle's central computer? That you haven't been able to find the verbal input codes for unlocking vital information . . . that I alone possess? That's why you were looking for me so desperately, Murasaki, and that's why it is so vital that I should not be found."

A defiant alien started to run forward, to protest. Sugihara-Fieh Chan cut him down with a single stroke of his sword.

"Well, let me tell all of you the story of my life." The silence in the room was total now; from outside, the sounds of fighting seemed infinitely distant. "On our homeworld there exists an ancient faith called *preta-na-ma*. It pertains to the belief in peace and brotherhood of all species. It encompasses many mysteries; its adepts, in the legendary past, were able to attain transcendent mental states in which they appeared to possess astounding powers. When the present, highly militaristic regime took over our planet centuries ago, and began forging its empire of savage cruelty throughout this sector of the galaxy . . . the old strong faith went underground. But it was still practiced in secret . . . passed down, in its fragmentary form, from teacher to pupil through the ages. And I, a young novice of *preta-na-ma*, heard tell of a distant planet that was being opened up for exploitation by our forces. A planet on which there existed religions that preached many of the precepts of *preta-na-ma:* and one in particular—Zen Buddhism— which shared many tenets and disciplines with it. I was inspired by this discovery; I had to see its true meaning for myself. It is to this end that I sought a command in the Visitor hierarchy . . . a position of power for which I was often compelled to compete in a most un*preta-na-ma*-like way. I came to this planet with many preconceptions. I thought that the earth creatures could be little more than animals, and this *preta-na-ma* of theirs but some tawdry mimickry of our own, true, ancient, buried ideals. I learned otherwise. I learned that there is goodness and compassion at the heart of all species . . . no matter that it has been repressed and beaten down for centuries in my own kind! For months I visited the great swordmaster Kenzo Sugihara. He taught me the way of the warrior; he taught me also the arts of peace. When I fell from the sky, wrapped only in my pressure skin, he was waiting for me, and in his mistress' laboratory he helped me fashion a second human visage for myself; for I had to be reborn. I could not be Fieh Chan for now . . . how could I bear to be a symbol of all that men loathed, the leader of the conquerors? It was only after he had rescued me that Sugihara revealed to me his intention of committing suicide in response to a demand from Lady Murasaki that he participate in a diabolical plan to train thousands of fighters to become soulless killing machines.

Sadly, because I had accepted his philosophy, I could not escape his consequences. I was asked to be his second in this act of *seppuku,* and I saw to it that Sugihara died correctly, elegantly and nobly. Yet I had doubts. Would I, in my previous days, have had the courage to end my own life rather than live in shame? I knew that I had to fight to protect the new way of life I had embraced. So, knowing what I knew about Murasaki's plans, I went to America and began to try to track down the masters of martial arts that they were planning to abduct . . . and here I am."

"What impertinence!" Murasaki said. "You are vastly outnumbered! And even if you kill those present, do you think you can continue for long? Soon your thermal pressure skins will no longer even be necessary! And the Mother Ships will return, Fieh Chan. You'll be taken back, court-martialled—if someone doesn't summarily execute you first—and punished severely."

At that point Matt, Rod and CB and a dozen other ninjas came bursting, weapons drawn, into the hall. Tomoko saw how Matt was bleeding, his cheek was gashed. She cried out his name. His lizard skin was hanging loose from his face; only patches of CB's remained. A scratching, ratchety sound against the walls outside . . . then they saw more ninjas, enemy ones, climbing in through the balcony window. Swords were out and swinging now.

"Stop! I command you, I, Fieh Chan!" Fieh Chan shouted.

"Who the hell is that?" Matt screamed, as his sword sliced off an alien hand and CB, diving between a lizard's legs, escaped being cut in two.

"That's Fieh Chan, but he's also Sugihara—I don't have time to explain!" Tomoko screamed as Murasaki wrested free, punched a larger hole in the shoji wall, clawed around, and pulled out a samurai sword! Quickly Tomoko fired blindly. The sword splintered against a bolt of blue lightning, and Murasaki cursed.

"Well, who's side is he on?" Matt shouted over the hubbub.

"Ours, I think!" Tomoko shouted back, firing at anything that seemed to want to attack her.

Above the tumult, Fieh Chan shouted out a few harsh words in the alien speech—

Walls moved behind them! Closets were flung wide to reveal a computer console with monitors and keyboards with bizarre hieroglyphs! Fieh Chan moved toward the console, his hands upraised, uttering more sounds in their language . . . but to Tomoko's surprise they were less grating than she had ever heard before; there was a kind of austere music to them, though she could not of course understand them.

Next to the computer console was a low table with votive objects and with a small Buddha image that seemed familiar to Tomoko. Yes, she had seen it before somewhere.

Tomoko went up to Fieh Chan's side. Rod, Matt, and CB, their swords trained on the enemies, joined them.

Fieh Chan said: "Since you failed to find a way to destroy the red dust, Murasaki, you sought instead to filter it out. The filtration system of this castle is not terribly effective, though you had to knock out most of the electrical power in this section of the country to do it. When someone is exposed, they still die . . . but even more painful and agonizingly than if they had simply succumbed immediately to the full dosage! I tell you this now because you are all going to experience it soon—"

"Nonsense! We are wearing the thermal pressure skins you yourself invented!" Murasaki said defiantly.

"But, my dear would-be rival," Fieh Chan said, and there was a hint of sadness in his voice, "what has been given can be taken away . . . and I had plans for such a contingency. There is in this castle's heating ducts, keyed to this computer and to my voice alone . . . a system for releasing an enzyme into the atmosphere . . . an enzyme that will dissolve the pseudo-protoplasmic bonds that hold my thermal pressure skins together! That enzyme has already been released . . . it will take effect in minutes!"

"Nonsense! It's a bluff! Even you, Fieh Chan, are not so callous as to betray your own people!"

"I have not betrayed them! On the contrary, I have exercised principles basic to my people's culture—principles suppressed for centuries, which yet hold true!" He spoke to Tomoko now. "That Buddha," he said. "You know what to do."

She remembered now. There had been one just like it in Fieh Chan's bedchamber, the day she had been brought before him. She lifted it gingerly from the low table. At once another wall peeled wide and she saw that beyond it lay a secret docking bay like she had been in once before, on the Mother Ship.

Two or three skyfighters were there for the taking. "Quick!" Tomoko shouted. They ran for the nearest one, their swords and guns still pointed at the assembly.

Fieh Chan refused to step on the shuttlecraft with them.

"Why?" Matt said. "You've done so much, and if you stay here—"

"You'll die," CB said. And Tomoko saw that the kid was on the verge of tears.

"I must die," Fieh Chan said. "I have betrayed my people. And it was not entirely out of noble causes that I did it. I was also sustained by . . . a strong feeling . . . for a woman of an alien species . . . one that I knew I could never truly have. Tell me, Tomoko . . . did you not love me? Even a little?"

She felt Matt's hands clutching her arms, warm and strong. She knew that Matt's love would always be with her. She began to weep, the tears running freely down her cheeks, like sweat . . . "Yes," she whispered. "Yes, I was tempted, Fieh Chan." And she knew also why the alien swordmaster had committed himself to die. He did not want to come between them. Because of this sacrifice, he was giving Matt and Tomoko the gift of a new chance, a renewed love.

"You must go now!" Fieh Chan drew his sword and stood straight, the blade catching the glow of the artificial lights in the banqueting hall. "They're coming after you. Into the hatch, quick! I'll try to fend them off. Up, up!" Then: *"Sayonara* . . . farewell, my temptress ape. . . .*"

Choking back her tears, Tomoko leaped into the sky-fighter and dashed for the controls.

"She knows how to fly this thing?" Rod said, awed, as he, CB and Matt scrambled in after her.

"My wife is very smart," Matt said proudly.

"Look!" CB yelled, pointing out of the windows, where they saw—

Dozens of aliens, beating each other out of the way in their haste to reach the remaining two skyfighters and avoid their impending death! They were no longer taking sides; it was a mad free-for-all as they jammed into the skyfighters, kicking each other on and off in their frenzy.

"No time to watch!" Tomoko said, as she pushed the button that sent them crashing into the night.

"They're coming after us!" CB said.

"I'd better do some fancy manuevers," Tomoko said. "If I can figure out how!"

Chapter 27

"They're coming too fast!" CB said in panic as they zoomed through a layer of cloud. Matt felt his stomach churning as they curved abruptly. Around them: night over rural Japan. Below: the Castle dimly visible in the moonlight.

And behind them . . . skyfighters . . . gaining fast!

"Try ducking!" Matt said.

"I need your help," Tomoko said. "Here, hold these controls steady and watch the altimeter . . . that's *that* thing." Matt slid into place beside Tomoko. It was amazing, watching her adapt so easily to the alien craft after only two previous attempts at flying one . . . was it due to her culturally complex background, perhaps, making her more chameleonlike? He soon started to get the hang of it too. Together they dived sharply, leaving the two pursuers nosing the moon.

Lower, lower they climbed. . . .

"Look at the Castle!" CB shouted as they swooped down close enough to see the courtyard and the steps. "People are running amok . . . there are corpses everywhere . . . a lot of people are fleeing from the Castle, down the hill. . . ."

"Good, they're escaping that living hell inside," Rod said. "If we confused them enough with our conflicting commands, maybe their minds were jolted back into reality."

"I hope so."

They were streaming from the Castle like ants now, thousands of them.

"Careful! They're coming back now!" CB screamed.

There they came, diving down from the face of the moon—

They separated! The two skyfighters came bearing down from either side of them. Swiftly they jerked up to another level and—

"Doesn't this thing have lasers, or something?" Rod said. "We can't outrun them forever."

"Yes," Tomoko said. Somewhere aft there's a control—

CB had found it. "Looks like a video game . . . I can handle it."

"Go for it, kid!" Matt said.

CB quickly found the scanners and the computer tracking device and activated them. A volley of blue light lanced the night air—

"Missed!" CB said.

Just then a blast rocked them. Matt felt out of his chair and banged his arm on the floor. "Hold the altitude!" Tomoko shouted. He clawed at the console, trying blindly to find the right controls, screaming for Rod to help. Rod rushed over. All three of them were hunched over the console, trying to straighten out the skyfighter, while one of the enemy ships was bearing down on them.

"What about CB? Should he be alone with those lethal weapons?" Rod said.

"With all the practice he's had at 'Galaga'," Matt said, "it should be a breeze."

"I'm gonna blow them out of the sky," CB said, jabbing at the controls again—

A huge explosion filled the darkness! It opened out in the black night like an incandescent flower, fringing the clouds with gilt and silver. Matt watched it for a few seconds in awe. But they couldn't dawdle. The second skyfighter was rapidly approaching them, spraying them with spurts of laser fire that crackled in the air like the lightning bolts from a Frankenstein machine.

They soared! Caromed over the roaring starburst of the exploded vessel! Zigzagged above the Castle from which throngs of people were still escaping! "I can't throw it off!" Tomoko cried. "I can't lose it!"

"We'll have to gun it down," CB said. "Awesome!" He let fly. "Take that, lizard scum . . . it's a hit!"

Matt took a look in the aft scanners. "I can see the face of the pilot . . . it's Murasaki herself," he said.

"Wow! Like if I blow her away I can get on to the next level?" CB said, his finger dancing madly on the controls.

They were spiralling over Osaka Castle. The enemy ship was practically on top of them. Its fire was skidding along the sides of their own ship. If they didn't score a hit soon—

At that moment it happened. A tremendous beam of brilliant light burst from the laser cannon—was hurled up at Murasaki's skyfighter—fireworks now, as the ship shattered into a thousand flaming fragments and began to rain down on the Castle. The river of people seemed to accelerate. For a moment it seemed that nothing had happened except for a few pockets of ruddy glowing within the Castle compound. Then, all at once, the Castle seemed to burst into flames all over. Smoke poured skyward. Clouds of bricks were flung into the air. Some of the last people to get out fell prey to the Castle's destruction, though most seemed to have gotten away.

"We did it! We did it!" CB was hollering. He ran to Matt and Tomoko and it was all too much for him suddenly . . . he began to cry. He was just a small boy far from home, after all.

Matt held him and said, "I'll never complain about missing quarters again."

The kid winked at him through his tears and said, "Hey, dude, it's casual."

"Now the big question is," Tomoko said, "which way is America?" She began to laugh.

"We can take as long as we want looking for it now!" Matt said. "We'll have our second honeymoon in Hawaii . . . double back to Australia. . . ."

"Do you think our friend made it out OK?" Rod said.

"I don't know," Matt said. "Maybe he had something up his sleeve. It wouldn't surprise me to find him waiting in California for me with divorce papers ready to sign!"

"Now don't be mean," Tomoko said. "You know, that man loved me."

"How can you call him a man?" Rod said angrily. "He was one of them . . . a stinking lizard."

"I think," Matt said, "we can all take a leaf out of his *preta-na-ma* book. And I think that if to be human means . . . to have compassion for other creatures . . . to love goodness . . . to strive against evil, no matter where that struggle may lead you . . . then Fieh Chan fits that description as well as any human being I've ever known."

"That's a very wise thing you've said," said Tomoko gently. And kissed him softly on the lips.

"That doesn't mean he can fool around with my wife, though," Matt added.

Tomoko laughed.

The skyfighter made its way across the sky. They flew low, so that they could see the hillsides with their terraced paddyfields, silver-etched by the moon.

"It's not too bad to be Batman and Robin and all those characters after all, huh?" he said. "I mean, saving the universe every day before dinner. Look at that countryside."

"It's good to be together," Tomoko said.

"You know," Rod said, "maybe I won't bother with that electrified fence after all . . . just too much damned trouble, keeping the whole world out . . . might as well join them."

"Do you think it's true, what Tomoko heard them say?" CB said at last. "That there may be a way of defeating the red dust, that the Mother Ships may soon return?"

"I don't know," Matt said. "But we'll be ready for them. When we stop off in Tokyo we're going to tell Setsuko and Dr. Schwabauer all that's happened, so the Japanese will be ready and waiting."

"Why can't we just go home?" said CB.

"Because our friend didn't tell which of these doodads is the compass," Tomoko said. "Remember, I always had Sugihara to tell me the way before. Besides, maybe we should turn over this thing to them so their scientists can study it . . . maybe even copy it. Then we'll *really* be ready for them if they return."

Matt said, "Besides which . . . maybe we can get some tourist sort of stuff done."

"What about my homework?" CB said, although Matt could tell he was only asking rhetorically, out of some kind of sense of duty.

"I for one," Rod Casilli said, "will be glad to get to Tokyo. The swill they've been feeding us prisoners at Osaka Castle was incredible! I probably wouldn't have eaten it if I'd known what was in it."

"Ah," Tomoko said. "You're ready for some nice raw fish?"

"Hell, no. I can't wait to get to Tokyo so I can get a decent hamburger!"

Watch for

THE CRIVIT EXPERIMENT

next in the V series
from Pinnacle Books

coming in May!